Meet Sachiko . . . so lively and pretty with her short-cropped hair and smart, Western dress . . . so young, so carefree and so in love. How could she know the price of such a love?

Could her love survive her humiliation? How far could she bend without breaking? Could she survive?

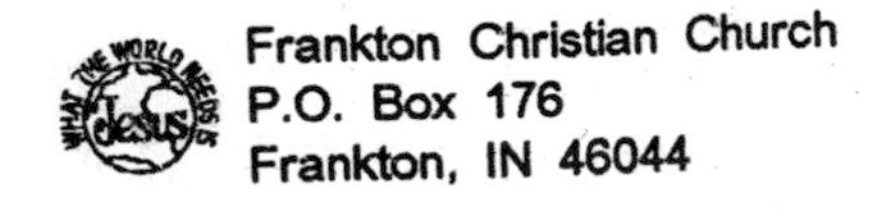

DAUGHTER IN BONDAGE

PHYLLIS KINLEY

WARNER PRESS • Anderson, Indiana

This is an entirely fictional book and no reference to actual persons is intended.

DAUGHTER IN BONDAGE

A PORTAL BOOK
Published by Pyramid Publications for Warner Press, Inc.

Portal edition published April, 1974

Library of Congress Catalog Card Number: 61-10354

ISBN: 0-87162-171-1

Printed in the United States of America

PORTAL BOOKS are published by Warner Press, Inc.
1200 East Fifth Street, Anderson, Indiana 46011, U.S.A.

Key to Japanese Pronunciation

The Japanese language has only one sound for each vowel: *a* as in *father; e* as in *they;* i as *ee* in *meet; o* as in *old; u* as in *food; ai* as in *aisle*. Doubling a vowel lengthens the sound without changing its quality: *oo* is long-drawn-out *o; aa* is like the *aa* in *baah; ii* like *ee-ee.* The consonants are pronounced much as in English, and each is followed by a vowel, except for *n* and *m* which may stand alone at the end of a syllable; *tsu* and *chi* are each one syllable—*ch* being sounded as in *chin.*

San is a title meaning "Mr.," "Mrs.," or "Miss." *Sensei,* which means "teacher," suggests respect. *Chan* is a title used in speaking to a child.

Japanese nouns have no plural forms. Thus *kimono* and *obi* are either singular or plural according to context.

CHAPTER ONE

SHE SLID THE DOOR shut gently and remained half kneeling as she looked about the room. "He's not here," she said to herself, and then walked slowly to the open window. Her feet, still damp from the bath, felt cool against the mat floor. In the dusk of the garden below, a mass of fireflies dipped almost to the surface of the water in the pond, hung there for a moment, and then darted off into the tall grasses of the far-off meadow.

"Hotaru koi . . . hotaru koi," she sang softly, her voice husky with the mystery that comes with twilight. "Come, fireflies. . . . The water here is sweet." She caught her breath, cautiously thrusting out her hand, for as if he heard her call, one tiny lantern broke from the whirling congregation of fireflies and danced toward her. "Come, firefly," she coaxed again, then fell silent when his burnished light was snuffed out. Strangely saddened, she sat looking out across to the river where his brothers whirled in never-ending frenzy. "Do they not know that one of them has left the family?" she wondered.

Suddenly she felt the soft caress of his tiny wings on her fingertips. A bittersweet pang of joy ran through her body, and she held him until he flew away again to the river. *"Sayonara,"* she called softly. "Good-by, little friend."

She closed her eyes. The garden was no longer there. She was a child again, hunting fireflies with her mother and brothers. They had returned from the riverbank in the dusk of the evening, their white cotton kimonos mussed and damp with perspiration, but their small bamboo insect cages had been bright with the light of the fireflies they had caught. She could almost feel the soft river grasses giving way beneath her feet, then springing up behind her as she passed.

She stood in the window of the hotel waiting for her husband and felt the same excitement she had felt that summer day so long ago. She remembered the sound of the rushing water and the dipping and turning of the lines upon lines of twinkling fireflies. And again, the song they had sung as they walked rang through her memories, *"Hotaru koi . . . hotaru koi . . ."*

Opening her eyes, she stood just a moment longer looking down into the garden, and then she turned and drew the paper and wood *shoji* closed. A flick of her slender wrist and the lamp on the low dressing table went on. She knelt in the pool of light and rearranged her hair. Then she powdered the back of her neck where the cotton kimono stood out stiffly. Dark eyes! Dark eyes set in a pale face looked back at her from the mirror; dark eyes and pale face framed in a circle of light. She tore her eyes away from her image and glanced again at the door.

"He's not here," she said aloud, and was startled at the sound of her voice. The stillness of the room swallowed it. As if rebuked, like a child who has been disciplined, she sat in her corner and waited, her dusky lashes downcast against pale cheeks.

When the door opened and he came into the room, she rose and took his soap and towel. Her hand trembled, and she turned away quickly so that he would not notice.

"How was your bath?" she asked.

He paused a moment before answering her. She felt his eyes, felt them travel over her neck, her carefully combed hair, the gay obi tie at her back.

When at last he spoke, his words came slowly, almost as if he had forgotten her question. "The bath? Hot! Really hot! I was lucky to be the first one down there."

He watched her as she opened the *shoji* and hung the wet towel on the small balcony railing.

"It's best to go down early in the evening—before the hikers come back," she said thoughtfully, turning to kneel beside the low table. "The water is always hotter then." They sat in silence for a while. "I asked the maid to bring our dinner. It should be here soon."

Perspiration appeared on his forehead. He turned the wide sleeves of his cotton kimono up and over his shoulders, leaving his arms bare to the slight breeze which came into the room from the garden. "I'm hungry," he said and folded his legs informally before him; ". . . sleepy, too. Baths always make me sleepy."

She smiled. Her face lost its tension and softened when she looked at him. "A bath feels good after a long train ride," she said. He did not answer. She watched his face, noting the strong masculine lines of his nose and chin.

"I was thinking of my father," he said at last. "We stayed in a hotel like this one time when I was a child."

She sat motionless, her hands clasped in her lap. From outside the window came the sound of a man's voice, then a woman's soft laughter. "You must have cared for him very much."

He paused and considered before answering. "I was so young when he was killed that I don't remember a great deal about him. But I do know that life was very different before the war came." He was silent for a long time.

"We waited for him to come home," he said finally. "I would dream of the day, planning each thing I would do and each word I would say. One day when I was returning from school, I thought I saw him walking up the street toward our house. It was raining and I ran, the water splashing over my clothes and into my boots. He had my father's shoulders, the same kind of military uniform, and he walked like my father. I thrust my hand into his. He clasped it strongly and turned toward me. But the face I saw was the face of a stranger. I had never seen him before."

She sat, scarcely breathing, her eyes fixed on his face.

"It was then that I knew my father was dead," he continued softly. "Toward the end of the war, a friend of my father's came to tell us of his death. My mother did not cry, but her eyes no longer laughed. She rocked me in her arms and said, 'Always remember, Ichiro Chan, that no matter where you may be, no matter what you may be doing, your father will be with you. He will be your guardian. Now he will be able to take better care of you than if he had lived.' "

The stillness of the early evening spread into their room from the rest of the hotel and from the garden. The girl's head was bowed and her hands were clasped loosely in her lap.

The silence was broken abruptly when the outer door of the room opened, and amidst a clatter of dishes, the hotel maid called out for permission to enter.

"Hai, dozo," the man answered.

There was a whispered conversation behind the inner door, then a smothered giggle. The girl's face flushed slightly and she avoided the eyes of the man.

He glanced self-consciously at his young wife and his face darkened. "Come on! Bring it in!" he ordered curtly, almost crudely. The whispering stopped abruptly and the inner door opened.

The maid, a heavy-set country girl, set the heavy tray on the mat floor and placed the dishes on the table. Her face was flushed with exertion, and beads of perspiration clung to her forehead.

"What do you want to drink? Beer? Sake?" She sank back on her heels and waited for their answer. Her eyes, impudent and bold, examined the girl's kimono, her short-cut hair and white face.

"Bring us two bottles of cider," he answered shortly. The maid flushed, and turning quickly, left the room.

He glanced half-ashamedly at the girl. "What a stupid maid! It's unusual to find one like that in a good hotel."

She smoothed the cotton of her kimono, self-consciously keeping her eyes from his until she knew they would no longer betray her. Then she raised them bravely to his and smiled a little, embarrassment still bathing her cheeks with pink. "It's all right," she said simply. "It's all right."

They ate their dinner quickly—the rice, the clear soup, boiled vegetables, the fish, vinegared vegetables and relishes, and last of all a large white peach. Once their eyes met across the table, and there was no longer need for words between them. It was as if the last few hours of the wedding, the trip by train, the arrival at the hotel, and the constrained silence before and after the bath were forgotten. She leaned over to refill his cup of tea, aware of his eyes following her movements. Then quietly, she chose a peach from the fruit dish, peeled it carefully, cut it in pieces and offered it to him. She responded to the message in his eyes and in return offered the best of everything—the choicest peach, the most comfortable cushion, herself—even though she might be unsure of his love for her.

They fled from the hotel to the quietness and darkness of the mountainside. They walked in the cool of the summer evening without talking. Then, as silently as they had gone, they entered the hotel and went separately to the baths again. Before she left their room, she slipped off the heavy obi tie from around her waist and removed the beautiful flowered summer kimono, putting on, instead, a plain one laid out by the hotel maid. Then, carrying her soap and towel, she walked along the narrow corridors to the women's bath.

How kind he is, she thought. In some ways he is very traditional, but in other ways he is so modern. She smiled as she pushed open the door to the bath.

The dressing room was empty. When she had been in the bath earlier that day it had been full, and the noisy, chattering voices of the women had resounded from wall to high wall. She slipped off her clothes, placed them in a bamboo basket on a stand, and taking her soap and towel, went into the inner bathroom.

With a ceiling so high that the steam from the water hid it from view, it was even so not a large room. The floors and walls were tile. Stacked beside the wall under the water faucets, were wooden buckets. Beyond the white expanse of tile lay the pool-like bath and beyond that a curved and moss-covered rock protruded from the wall, giving the appearance of a garden. One small, gnarled and twisted pine tree grew from the rock, clung tenaciously to the moss, its roots washed constantly by a waterfall cascading from the ceiling.

She quickly washed at the side of the room, then poured buckets of water from the bath over her body, causing the steam to rise even more thickly around her. The water in the bath was hot, hotter than it had been earlier. Carefully, making as little movement as possible, she slid into the pool and knelt on the bottom so that the water rose to her neck.

She found that when she moved, her body tingled with the heat, but when she remained still it became a warm blanket that soothed and relaxed every muscle. The sound of the water running constantly lulled her half asleep.

So much has happened in the last few weeks, she thought. To think that six months ago I did not even know him! She spoke his name tentatively several times . . . "Ichiro . . . Ichiro . . ." It re-echoed in the empty room so loudly that, even though she was alone, she blushed and spoke aloud no more.

Her father had mentioned the names of several of his friends' sons, but she had not been interested enough to assent to an *omiai*—a meeting. She had not felt that she was ready to marry so soon after university graduation, but her mother worried lest she should wait too long and perhaps lose the chance to make a good marriage.

Three or four times her father had said casually that Kawaguchi Sensei, a doctor friend of his, knew of a young man of good background who was interested in finding a bride.

Sachiko had refused to meet the man because she had already met the Kawaguchi family and had not liked them. "That woman is a hypocrite," she had said to herself when she first saw them talking to her parents on the street. "Her face is filled with false sympathy and understanding, no deeper than her skin. As for the man—he is a weakling!" She dismissed them from her mind, never dreaming that not too much later they would play such an important part in her life.

"Sachiko," her father had said one night after leaving his office, "you know we would never force you to marry anyone you did not want to marry."

His eyes when he looked at her held a special light which they never held for anyone else. The smell of antiseptic and medicines which always seemed to permeate his clothing spoke of greatness to her—a greatness which was associated with her father alone. She noted fleetingly that his eyes, while alert, looked tired and his face was drawn and pale. She was under no illusions. She knew she was her father's favorite, especially since Toshiro had died. Taro would always be the heir, but she knew that her father's love was hers.

"I know you wouldn't, Father," she answered gently, "but I don't want to marry someone whom I do not like."

"You've read too many foreign novels," he laughed, but his eyes remained serious. "This is my reward for sending you to the university to study English! But Sachiko, remember that love usually comes after marriage if it is a good match. How are you going to find whether you like someone or not if you don't meet him?" He reached into his pocket and drew out a photograph. "Kawaguchi Sensei gave this to me."

She took it silently. It was a picture of a young man,

tall and good-looking, dressed in a Western suit. His face was strong and proud. His lips, narrow and sensitive, held a hint of a smile that seemed to know it should not be there but could not help itself. Reluctantly she had to admit to herself that she would have to look far before she would find a man as impressive as was this one. She especially noticed his eyes—large and wide open with a direct, searching gaze. She dropped the picture on the table.

"His family were samurai," her father's voice went on, quietly, carefully. "He is an only son and supports his mother. Kawaguchi Sensei said that his wife is a personal friend of the young man's mother and that they know the family well. They recommend him highly." He glanced at her quickly. "Would you meet him, Sachiko?"

She thought the matter over. "I'll meet him, Father," she said at last. "But I don't want anything elaborate planned."

"Perhaps just a meeting at Kawaguchi Sensei's home?"

"No, I don't want to go there."

"A play, then? And afterward go somewhere to eat."

"Let's just meet for dinner."

"I'll talk with Kawaguchi San tomorrow, then." He left the room, and they did not mention it again that day.

"Sachiko, wear your new kimono," her mother said to her the morning of the meeting—the *omiai*. "Kawaguchi San told your father that the man's family is very traditional. A kimono will make a better impression."

"Oh, Mother, do you think so?" Doubtfully, Sachiko lifted the kimono out of the drawer of her chest and lay it on the floor beside a pale blue sweater. When they lay on the mat floor together it was difficult to decide which to use—the one so traditional, the other so modern. "I like to wear a kimono," she said, "and his mother would probably like the kimono best." But her eyes strayed to the soft wool, hesitated lovingly over the tiny flowers set in pink at the neck.

Her hand then reached into a desk near by and drew out the picture. Silently, she studied it. Suzuki San . . . Suzuki Ichiro . . . is it to be you for whom I will leave my family and friends, my mother, my room here in a home where I am loved, my father who loves me more than his sons? What are you? Are you kind? Will you treat me gently? If we marry, will love come afterward? Or will you be impatient and demanding? Will you listen to what I have to say? Wryly, she placed the picture on the mat floor before her. There were not many men as wise and kind as her father, she thought.

Her hands hovered indecisively above the pink kimono, lifted it, and held it against her. I know how I would look in this, she thought. I would not have to worry about my appearance. "But what do I care!" she cried aloud angrily, laying it down roughly beside the blue sweater. "Do I care what they think?"

Suddenly, she knew she did care, deeply and honestly. She remembered the calm strong look of the man's jaw and the quirk of a smile at the corner of his mouth. I care what he thinks, she thought with surprise. And without thinking, while a strange excitement rose in her body, she pushed the kimono aside and reached out to the sweater.

They met in front of the restaurant. He is tall, she thought after one stolen glance. Taller than I had expected. His hair was slightly curly, lending boyishness to his face. Yet the firm jaw and the direct gaze told her that he was a man—a man who had confidence in himself and his abilities. His mother stood between him and the go-between, the two of them talking with the intimacy of old friends. Sachiko's eyes passed quickly over the gushing sweetness of Kawaguchi San's wife. A slight revulsion swept her as she dismissed the woman from her mind and directed her attention instead to the mother.

Dark hair drawn back in a bun, her eyes narrow and

bright, Yoshiko Suzuki still carried a slight trace of the beauty that had been hers years before. But her lips had lost the softness they had held then, and her face was pale and tight. Clothed in a dark conservative kimono and coat, standing quietly beside her son, she nevertheless gave an unmistakable impression of power and aggressiveness.

"Now be careful, Sachiko," her mother warned as they drew near to the place where the three stood. "Don't talk too much."

I couldn't if I wanted to, thought Sachiko, trying to still the frantic beating of her heart. All during the introductions she was aware of the man's mother; she knew that there was little that she did that missed the attention of the older woman. The man, Ichiro Suzuki, after a brief look at her face, seemed unaware of her presence and talked with the go-between in a relaxed manner. Then, formal greetings completed, they walked into the restaurant, Sachiko and her mother a step or so behind the others.

After the wedding she was to remember little of their conversation that day nor could she recall the food they ate. But she remembered the difficulty she had in answering the simple questions the mother asked her. Her hands trembled while they ate, and she controlled them only by pressing them together under the table. She remembered little things, unimportant things, such as the amount of food Ichiro ate, the way he smiled in answer to remarks made by the go-between, the smart masculine smoothness of his Western suit. Through it all, his mother's examining eyes burned like a brand upon her memory. Then she was sorry that she had not worn the kimono, for she had begun to sense almost unconsciously, that in this case it was more important to impress the mother than to impress the son.

Voices in the outer room brought her back with a start to the bath and the hotel. She climbed out of the bath, wiped her reddened body with a small towel and slid open the door into the dressing room. Three women looked at her curiously when she came into the room, but as she turned her back to them and began dressing quickly, they forgot that she was there, and their voices rose again like the twittering of birds.

When she entered her sleeping room the lights were turned off, and only the small lamp beside the dressing table still burned. The heavy shutters were drawn against the night air and the *futon* mattresses were spread on the floor. In the dimness of the room she did not see him at first.

"Sachiko!"

Sleepily, her body numbed by the warm bath, by shyness, perhaps even by fear, she turned toward him and sat obediently on the edge of his *futon*. For the first time a shadow of uncertainty—of shyness—passed over his face making him seem younger than his years. When she saw it her fear left her, and her hand reached out to meet his.

Outside the frogs still cried in the night, and the fireflies still played hide and seek among the dusky trees in the garden. Someone in a room near by began to sing, accompanied by the mournful tones of a *samisen*.

"Sachiko," he said again, more strongly than before.

The light in the lamp flickered and then burned steadily, answering the smile in the girl's eyes.

CHAPTER TWO

THE SOUND OF BIRDS woke her the next morning. Sachiko stretched her hand out from under the *futon,* pushed the pillow to one side and lay with her eyes half shut. Above the alcove in the room was a carving that reminded her of her parents' home—a piece of wood that twisted and turned into a full circle, then, smooth and polished, melted into the wall. The birds chirped again outside the shuttered windows. Her eyes closed and she slept.

Suddenly she was in her father's house again. It was late afternoon. The sun flowed richly into the guest room from the garden outside and was reflected in the polished, curving wood carving. She touched the part of it that ran down the side of the alcove, her fingers fitting into the smooth grooves as they so often had since she first crept about the room.

She dreamed she was a child again, her skirts short above her bare legs, her hair bound into braids that reached below her waist. The sound of birds mingled with the clucking of her chickens outside the veranda. From the kitchen came the noise of pans rattling and the smell of charcoal. Mother was preparing dinner. She sat quietly thinking of the chickens . . . and of the grasshoppers she must catch to feed them so that they might grow fat and give eggs.

Tomorrow before I leave for kindergarten, she thought, I must get up early and catch some more. Forgetting the carving, she stepped lightly over the warm mat floor, then the still warmer wood floor of the veranda, and into the wooden split-toed clogs which lay on the graveled path.

The closely pruned trees in the garden cast long, lean shadows on the ground. Skirting the pond where the golden fish swam, eager for a bite of bread for their afternoon snack, she reached the chicken cage. There she stopped, her breath caught in wonder. For in the center of a large pile of straw, like a miniature *daruma* doll which has no legs—like a very fat little king in the center of a very large pillow—lay an egg! A creamy white, though very small, egg! To Sachiko it was the best gift she had ever received, for it was the first egg her chickens had given her. Proudly she bore it to the kitchen, and that evening it was set in the place of honor—on the god-shelf. It became food for the gods! To Sachiko, who ate it later, it was the tastiest food she had ever eaten.

She woke again, stirred and lay drowsily thinking of her father's house, of her father's office in the front of the house, and the smell of antiseptics that filled the house when he treated his patients there. She thought of her mother who served the family quietly day after day, of her grandmother who ruled the home, of her noisy and spoiled younger brother Taro, and of her older brother Toshiro who died in the war. But her love had been most of all centered in her father. It was he who carried her on his back for long walks when she was a tiny child. He had allowed her to play in the fascinating office. He had brought her candy or toys whenever he returned from a trip.

Mornings, when she was four and five years old, she had spent in a near-by kindergarten. There, dressed in a blue-smock uniform, she learned to sing and play with the other children. She had especially liked folding paper. During the lesson she loved to sit beside the teacher and often watched her fold paper into different shapes long after her friends had tired of it and run to play. Yellow paper cranes, a red boat, blue and white flowers—she had saved them for a long time in a little box, bringing them out to look at on special occasions.

She spent hours playing in the sandbox at the kindergarten, building sand castles, carrying water to make moats around them, and tearing them down to begin again. Even in the coldest days of winter she played there, her hands growing chapped and raw from the cold and her cheeks turning pink. Then, after two years of playing and studying, she had dressed in her kindergarten smock with a white handkerchief in its pocket and, bowing three times, had received her diploma from the white-gloved hands of the principal. Her mother had wept and her father had tried to appear very unconcerned although she knew he was proud of her.

Near her home was a small Shinto shrine of plain, unpainted wood. It was set in the midst of tall pine trees, under which grew wild flowers and grasses. Every morning the people of the community would gather there to do exercises to music on the radio. Often she would go with her father to join them, enjoying the morning air and the experience of being with older people. Sometimes her father would take her to the primary school grounds, and she would play on the swings or watch the older boys play baseball.

One year before the great war ended, the bombings became so heavy that all the primary school children were ordered to leave together for a temporary living place in the country. Her mother did not want her to be separated from her family completely, and so took her instead to a cousin of hers who lived in a little village about two hours' train ride from their home in Tokyo. She and her mother lived in the quiet countryside for eight months and spent their time helping her cousins in the fields and about the farmhouse. It was a large old-fashioned farmhouse with a thatched roof and a wide veranda. The family storehouse stood to the west of the house, and in the courtyard was a garden where a few chrysanthemums remained. Under the eaves of the thatched roof hung persimmons, strung on strings like huge orange pearls. Beside them swung ears of corn and two-feet-long white radishes, drying in the winter sun.

Occasionally they heard the sound of airplanes, but none came as far as their village. Her father came to visit one Sunday a month. Then she would walk along the country road to the river with her father and mother, stop once in a while to watch a bird or to call to a friend, but all the time listening intently to what her father had to say. Her mother would interrupt him time after time: "How is Grandmother getting along? Is she sleeping well?" Or she might say quietly, "Have you heard from Toshiro?"

In the years that followed, Sachiko thought often of her brother and of his death. And when she thought of him, she also had to think of her people and of her country. She remembered the old men who had gathered around the country cousins' hearth on a cold winter afternoon. Crouching in a dark corner of the large, drafty house, she had listened to their talk. A small, lithe girl-child, she would not have been noticed even if she had sat with them around the warmth of the coals or drank with them from the cups of hot tea poured from a large iron teapot.

She remembered how they had peered at each other over their round, thick glasses or stroked their straggly beards and solved all the problems of the country. They told the old stories of days gone by—of the days when Japan had been the victor, when other countries had felt her power. And without fail they told of the Mongolian ships which even with guns had failed in their mission of conquering the beautiful islands of Japan. They talked of the brave Japanese archers who, knowing that they could not hope to win against the mightiest armada in all Asia, had prayed for a miracle and when it had come had fallen on their knees in thanksgiving to the gods who had sent it. The "winds of the gods"—the kamikaze, the storm—had suddenly struck and destroyed the Mongolian ships, sending them home stricken and broken and in shame.

The old men had laughed triumphantly, "Again, as in days of old, the winds of the gods will save us! The kamikaze will not let us be conquered!"

It had all seemed so false—so futile. On the one hand, here were the old men who read their history books and sat by the *hibachi* and cackled as they drank strong tea, and who knew all the answers! On the other side, obscured by time, yet glorified by it, stood her older brother Toshiro, who left his country one dark night on a mission and who never returned.

The "winds of the gods" did not save him. He died for his country, a kamikaze suicide pilot, somewhere in the middle of the Pacific Ocean.

The war ended while they were yet in the country. Neighboring farmers, clad in black ceremonial kimono with the white round crest of their family, the only mark setting them apart from each other, gathered in her cousins' best room to listen to the Emperor speak to them on the radio. For a long time after the Emperor told them of the unconditional surrender, there was silence in the village. Although only a child, Sachiko crept into the storehouse, and with her hand over her mouth so no one could hear her, she wept without knowing just why she was weeping.

She stirred restlessly, wiped the tears and perspiration from her face. Still half asleep, she rose, pushed open the shutters and stood looking outside. Why should I cry over something that happened so long ago, she wondered. It's bad luck to cry on one's honeymoon.

Cradled in the valley by tall mountains, the hotel lay quietly hushed in the morning air. A mountain stream beyond the meadow tried in vain to break the silence with the song of its rapids, but it seemed only to emphasize the quietness that lay about her. Luxuriant with growth, the mountains shut out the outside world and made her own world seem very small.

She turned from the window, but as she did so her eyes caught a glimpse of her young husband in the garden. "Come down. Come down," his eyes smiled at her, beckoned to her, waited for her. "Come down," his lips echoed. The ache forgotten, the past forgotten, everything forgotten except for the here and now, she hastened with her dressing, slipped on slim slacks and a white shirt, ran a comb quickly through her hair. As she did it she sang, keeping rhythm with the crazy beating of her heart.

He looks so nice, she thought as she walked toward him through the garden. His shoulders seemed broader still under the cotton kimono, his slender hips more slender. When he smiled down at her his eyes crinkled in the corners.

"I hated to wake you."

"You should have. It is a bad thing for a wife to stay in bed after her husband is up."

"Oh, but I am a modern husband." He used the English word.

She smiled. She knew not only that never again would she sleep late, but also that he would not want her to do so after the honeymoon.

The smile remained on her face as she walked to the edge of the garden and stood looking up at the mountain. Then it faded and a quietness descended upon her.

He followed and stood looking down at her. "It is beautiful."

"Yes, it is, isn't it," she answered dreamily, unaware of his real meaning. "And on the top I'd build a tiny house with a wide veranda and a garden."

"And walk down that mountain every day for vegetables and then back up again?" he queried with forced lightness.

"Perhaps I could build an elevator—one large enough for only me." She smiled quickly, her voice warming at his teasing. "But you could use it on alternate days!"

They laughed together. "After our breakfast, let's hike to the top," he said.

"Yes, to the very top."

For two hours they climbed steadily and without speaking. They paused only for a moment now and then to look out over the tops of the trees to the valley below. The path grew rougher and more narrow. Sometimes the trees and underbrush hid everything but the path from their eyes, and even that at times seemed to end in the thickness of the forest. But as they walked on it curved upward and continued on through the thickly wooded slopes of the mountain. The cedars and pine sent down their fragrance, and flowers covered the ground about their feet.

When they came closer to the top, the path became steeper. At times, a misstep would have dashed them to the slope below; at other times, they were completely surrounded by protecting trees. Ichiro turned once or twice, adjusted the thermos on his shoulder, and helped her find footing on the path; then once again, leading the way, he started carefully upward.

Suddenly the path widened, rounded a curve, and opened onto a level wooded plateau. There in simplicity, calling no attention to itself, stood a small Shinto shrine, its unpainted wood melting into the background of the trees and the mountainside. A small red *torii* marked the entrance from the path.

"Not very many people come this way," Sachiko said. "The cleansing fountain hasn't been cleaned for a long time." Tiny wooden dippers with long handles, bleached by the sun, rested unused beside the fountain. Dust lay on the floor of the shrine and on the wooden steps leading to it. A lone mound of rice, an offering of some poor farmer, was piled before the doorway. The large rectangular money box which guarded the entrance was empty.

Ichiro stood looking down into the valley. They could just see the tiled roof of the hotel. The river beyond was a narrow ribbon. Above them, a hundred yards or so, was the top of the mountain, treeless and barren. They rested in the quietness of the shrine, almost lulled to sleep by the warmth of the sun and the humming of the bees.

"The quiet spots always seem so different from the places we live," he mused. He stretched his legs over the wild grasses of the shrine garden and lay looking up at the sky. "But you will like Tachikawa, I think."

"I had been there only once before I met you," she said.

"Only once?"

"Yes. I went to visit a friend who lives there. Her husband works at the American Air Force Base."

"Many of the people who live in our community do," he said absently. "Where does your friend live?"

"Not far from your mother's home." She waited, thinking that she would tell him of her friend, Matsuoka, but when he did not reply, she, too, became silent.

A smile passed over his face. "I am eager for you to become well acquainted with my mother," he said finally. "Perhaps because of the death of my father, she has been closer to me than most mothers are to their sons."

She looked at him and smiled. "I want to know her well. Tell me about her." She sat beside him on the grass. Her eyes watched him expectantly.

He paused, then began to speak slowly. A slight frown appeared on his forehead and his eyes fixed in an unblinking stare on the faraway mountains. "When I think of my mother," he said, "I think of the war, for it was at that time that I really knew how much she loved me. I was only eleven in the summer of 1944 when I was evacuated with the rest of the children in my class at school, together with our teacher, to a resort in the mountains. The hotels were crowded with wounded soldiers and with children, hungry for food and for love they did not receive.

"It was a horrible place," he went on. "My parents were allowed to visit me only twice a year and even our letters were censored. We were homesick for our families and homes and this, together with the lack of good food, made us quarrelsome and ill-tempered." He paused and then went on bitterly, "Two of the stronger students, a girl and a boy, took advantage of this atmosphere and set up an organization to control the weaker children. I shall never forget the hatred of the boy chief. We dared not tell the teacher of the way he treated us, for his friends spied on us and life would have been unbearable. I was fortunate, for I became ill and my mother had to take me home again. How glad I was to see her!

"Bombings were now taking place every day. We could not stay in Tokyo, and since my father had already gone to war, my mother decided that she and I had better go to stay with the head family of the village where her people had previously lived." He stirred restlessly, remembering the terror of that day. "We stood in line for hours at Shinjuku Station, waiting for seats on a train. Schedules were forgotten since the trains could run only between air raids. But when we finally got a seat, it was only the beginning. I remember the children crying because every time we stopped in a tunnel to wait for the bombers to leave the smoke would sift into the train and hurt their eyes. But worse than that was the fear that when we did emerge from the tunnel the planes would return and kill us."

"It must have been difficult for your mother," Sachiko whispered wonderingly. She tried to think of Ichiro's mother as a young woman, but could not imagine her in any other way than bitter and cold. Some time before the war came, before her husband was killed and her home lost, she must have known joy. Sachiko sat sunk in her thoughts, trying to picture the young Mrs. Suzuki, but failed.

"It was hard for her," he said at length in a changed voice, low and slightly unsteady. "Sometimes she went to Tokyo to trade rice for kimonos and obis. Later she sold her own kimonos along with the ones she brought back from the city—sold them one by one so that we would have something to eat." For a long time he sat silent.

"She had been raised in the city," he said at last. "She had never worked on the farm before. But she learned to work in the fields and to draw carts with the other women. Never did I hear her complain. When my father was killed she only worked harder, since she knew that now she must make a way for me to live as well, but something in her died with him." His voice grew cold. In a sudden fierce movement he rose to his feet. "One night she did not return from Tokyo when she said she would come. When she finally arrived home the next day she was not the same as she had been when she left. Her train had been bombed as it left a tunnel. The experiences she had that night in the burning train changed her. It was as if her heart had died with the people she saw dying on the train."

He turned from Sachiko. Suddenly he had no need of her. He seemed not to know her at all. And she sat, drawn inside herself, shriveled with pain for him, as she watched him walk up the mountain to the bare, tree-deserted top. There he sat, removed from her, sunk in his own dark thoughts.

His mother! she thought to herself. He talks so much about her, almost as if he worshiped her. She searched her mind, tried to remember the things she knew about her new mother-in-law. Her courage in protecting Ichiro from danger in the war, her work in the small shop she began upon their return to Tokyo, her desire to help him complete his university training—all these things she tried to keep consciously in mind. But the face of his mother did not fit the picture of courage and love which he had painted for her. She recognized only bitterness and a cold, cold pride.

Sachiko walked to the small dusty shrine and stood looking into its dark interior. A pile of rice on the floor! Someone had come here to ask for help. Someone else came praying. Someone who may have felt as she did. Thinking of that person, her body and hands automatically took the same pose which the visitor's before her must have taken. Three hand claps, a prayer wafting through an empty shrine, three more claps. Above her the wind cried in the tops of the trees. And somehow the prayer escaped and brought her no satisfaction at all. The tension remained within her, a premonition of something dark, of some unhappiness to come.

Clouds suddenly covered the sun. The girl shivered and started up the hill to her husband.

CHAPTER THREE

TWO DAYS LATER THEY LEFT the mountains and returned to Tokyo. It was late afternoon when they stepped off the train at Tachikawa, walked off the platform and through the tunnel that led to the south side of the station. I'd forgotten how hot it is in the city, Sachiko thought, as she wiped the perspiration from her forehead. The blue cloth of the parasol she held above her head was as nothing in the face of the sun's heat. She quickened her steps, aware of her husband's relief at being almost home.

The street that led from the station was a wide one, crowded with housewives shopping for dinner and children returning home from a day of fishing and swimming in the river. They stepped aside often to let a car or truck pass by, then continued down the side of the street. After a short time they turned and entered a narrow side street, one shaded by trees and lined with private houses behind bamboo fences.

A housewife leaned out a window to call to them. "Suzuki San! *Okaeri nasai!* Welcome home!"

Ichiro stopped and bowed. *"Tadaima!"* Then smiling, "This is my wife. I have told her about our good neighbors already."

"So desu ka? We have looked forward to your return home." She smiled at Sachiko. "You must come to see us soon, *Okusan*. We have four noisy children who think a great deal of your husband. They will want to meet you, too."

"Thank you, I will be glad to come," Sachiko said quietly and bowed again.

"It's good to be home again," Ichiro said, as they left

the street for a footpath. "Mother will be glad to see us."

A tall bamboo fence, a gate with a sliding door—this was to be her new home, perhaps for the rest of her life. Sachiko slid the door shut and stood looking about her at the garden and the house. She had visited here twice before, once during the time the marriage arrangements were being made and once more when she brought her clothing and furniture shortly before the wedding. The stain on the house had long ago bleached into a lighter, more neutral shade, making it seem a part of the landscape of the garden. A small storehouse could be seen to the right of the house and beside it Ichiro's dog, Shiro, leaped up and down, wagging his tail so hard that his whole body moved and the chain that held him rattled against the wall of the doghouse.

"Tadaima," Ichiro called loudly. As he shoved the entrance door aside the bell above it danced and jingled madly.

"Okaeri nasai," a woman's voice answered from somewhere inside the house. Sachiko hardly had time to step into the entrance before her mother-in-law appeared. "Are you back already?" She took the bags Ichiro handed to her, placed slippers in the hallway for him, ignoring Sachiko who stood in the door. Still talking, the older woman carried the bags to their room, followed by her son.

Sachiko stepped up out of the entrance and knelt down to straighten the shoes—her own Western-type shoes, her husband's good leather ones, her mother-in-law's wooden *geta*. Then, hesitatingly, she stepped across the bare floor of the hall to the eating room and from there to the wide veranda that looked out into the garden. Beyond the eating room and also facing the veranda was the guest-living room with a large alcove on one side and a closet for bedding on the other. One door from the eating room led to the kitchen, she remembered.

Placing her purse on the low table in the eating room, she sat down on the mat floor. From the veranda came the cool tinkling of the *furin,* made of little else than glass, bright paper streamers, and strings, but so pleasant when hung in the breeze. Sachiko turned her eyes to the room, examined the books in the bookcase curiously. The books must be Ichiro's, she thought. Several of them were in English.

Her mother-in-law's voice could be heard clearly through the thin walls. It rose thin and high above the accompaniment of Ichiro's deeper tones. Suddenly Sachiko wished desperately that she could leave the house and walk down the road and back to her parents' home. The strangeness, the high-pitched chattering, the feeling of being a guest and yet not a guest bewildered her. She clenched her hands in her lap and waited for her mother-in-law's return.

"And then Yamaguchi Sensei from the high school called and asked for you, and I told him you would be back in a couple of days—it's something about a meeting. You had better go to see him tomorrow." On and on it went until Sachiko felt that she could stand it no longer.

"Mother, what about Sachiko?" It was a whisper but Sachiko heard it plainly.

"What did you say? Who?" Deliberately loud, her voice carried through the house and on out the window.

"Sachiko!"

"Oh, I completely forgot her. Sachiko!" There was the sound of steps in the hall. "Sachiko, come right in. We'll be out in a minute." She peered around the edge of the door. "Oh, I see. You are in already. Well, make yourself comfortable." Footsteps padded back to the other room. "Ichiro, why don't you wear this cotton kimono. The other one is too worn. You really need more than one. I'll have to see about getting you another. Now, as I was saying, Yamaguchi Sensei is . . ." Sachiko stood up abruptly and walked into the garden, using wooden clogs she found beneath the veranda.

A kitten played with a string in the sun, a tiny yellow ball of fur. She caught the string and pulled it, teasing the animal until it finally tired of playing and crawled up into her lap when she crouched on the ground beside it. She carried it with her to a stone bench and sat stroking its ears until it slept. She was tired, too. The quietness and warmth of the garden seeped into her body and her eyes closed. For just a moment she felt the tension leaving her and with it all anger and loneliness.

After dinner that evening, she sat in the six-mat corner room, the room which was to be hers and Ichiro's, and unpacked the things she had brought from her parents' home. Her husband and his mother still sat at the table in the family room, talking of people she did not know, of places she had never been. One window of her room looked out into the yard where Ichiro's little dog lay. She called to him softly and he cocked his head up at her, his ears standing straight up. She heard the soft thud, thud of his tail as it beat against the side of the storehouse.

The room was not large but was comfortable enough for sleeping two people. Against the wall she had placed her large chest, a wedding present from her father. Beside her lay a half-opened box full of books and papers and beyond that were her kimonos, tied in a four-cornered cotton *furoshiki*. She untied it and took out the kimonos carefully. There were three of them. She laid them in the bottom drawer of the chest, first the pink summer one, then the darker winter kimono, and last, the *homongi* which she used only for special occasions.

All evening she worked steadily, stopping occasionally to glance over old high school programs and photographs taken during the years she went to the university. She sat looking at the photograph album. Here was a picture of a foreign teacher she had for English study. There was another of a group of laughing girls. She laid the book aside and went on with her work, but her lips smiled and she thought for a long time of the carefree days which the book represented.

The last book, the last piece of clothing, the last note and paper had gone into her chest when she heard the heavy wooden shutters being closed in the other room. Then the bathroom door beyond the kitchen opened and closed and she knew that Ichiro had gone in to take his bath. She pulled aside the door to the closet, took out the bedding and laid it on the floor. It was new, brought with her from her home. Bright-red plaid mattresses, white sheets to cover them—the two beds lay side by side on the straw-matted floor. She undressed and put on her sleeping kimono.

The bathroom door opened. She heard her husband and mother-in-law talking for just a moment in the eating room, then the bathroom door opened and closed again. There was the sound of water being run, a pan banging on the wooden platform. She stood still, her breath coming shallow and quick. Then, her bare feet making no noise, she stole into the hallway and looked into the brightly lighted room. A clock ticking on top of the bookshelf, the sound of water splashing in the bath, the cicada's song coming from the tops of the trees—all brought a feeling of familiarity to the room.

The singing of the cicada lured her to the entrance. As if she were dreaming, her feet found wooden sandals and led her into the night. The garden was dark. The moon cast shadows upon the ground and twisted the shapes of the trees. Somewhere in the night a radio was playing a popular American hit tune. One of the shadows moved and she stopped, suddenly unsure, a little afraid.

"Ichiro?"

"Over here."

Her eyes adjusted to the darkness and she saw him clearly. A wave of happiness swept over her, sharp and sweetly painful. I belong to him, she thought. This man, his weakness and his strength, the strong direct gaze of his eyes, the quickness of his mind, his strong body and his dreams—I am a part of them all! She moved to his side and sat down by him on the stone bench. Her arm touched his.

He regarded her silently for a short while. "You've been neglected this evening."

"I've been busy, putting things away." She paused. Then hesitantly, "Do you think she will like me?"

"Of course she will. If you try to help her to do things her way." He looked away from the vulnerability of her face and into the safeness of the night. "Mother has never had a daughter, and it may be difficult for her to learn to have someone else share her home, but . . ." He stopped, then went on more strongly,"Of course, she will like you."

"Do you have to be gone tomorrow?"

"Yes, I have to see a teacher friend of mine about some business. School starts in September." He hesitated. "Look, Sachiko, you're going to have to learn to get along with Mother by yourself. I won't always be home, and you will have to face that fact sooner or later. It is better that you get it worked out right away."

"I will."

Silence. The night poured in upon them, warm and soft. Ichiro stirred, his arm reached around her and drew her against him. The softness of their kimonos lay between them, clean and intimate.

"Listen to the cicada! They are singing to us."

"I used to like to catch them when I was small."

"So did I. Sachiko?"

"Yes?"

"When Mother is done with her bath, you can take yours."

"Yes."

"And listen, probably you should take it upon yourself to clean it and to build the fire in it from now on. I wanted to tell you so Mother wouldn't have to do so tomorrow."

"Did she ask you to tell me?"

"No, but I'm sure she will want you to do it."

"I'll try to please her."

"I'm sure you will." Footsteps approached on the path. The clip-clop of *geta* marked the rhythm of the folk song their wearer was singing. Then slowly the song faded away, and more slowly still faded the sound of the wooden *geta*. The silence of the night returned and once again, from far in the distance, came the sound of the radio and an American popular tune. "Yamagata ken," he said musingly. "Yamagata—have you ever been there?"

"No, but it sounds beautiful."

"Some day, perhaps, we can go." His arm tightened around her. "But first we must have a child."

Aware of the moonlight on her face, she lowered her eyes, for she knew that he was watching her closely. She did not answer him at first, but in her heart she smiled. Feeling the warm flush that spread upward from her throat, she lifted her eyes shyly to his. "This first must be a girl, then a boy," she said.

He smiled, and she thought she saw her own joy reflected in his eyes. "I have always wanted a son to carry on our family name," he said.

"We will . . . some day we will."

He paused for a moment, then continued softly. "It is good to be here together, isn't it? I am happy. It seems as if the gods must have brought us together."

"I know."

"We must always be kind to each other," he said.

"Yes," she whispered.

They listened to the night. The sound of their breathing was loud in their ears, weaving a kind of spell about them.

But suddenly, breaking the magic stillness of the

night, came the voice of Ichiro's mother. "Ichiro, please lock the door after you come in."

His arm withdrew immediately from around Sachiko's waist. *"Hai, Okaasan!"* he answered.

"Then I'm going to bed," she persisted.

"Oyasumi nasai," the girl and the man called together.

He stood up abruptly, stretched, and started for the entrance door. "We must go in."

Automatically she rose to obey, her face smooth and untroubled. But her mind held a jumble of questions. Little by little she was finding the answers. "Sachiko, clean the bath! Mother won't have to tell you tomorrow. Do things her way . . . get along with Mother by yourself." Do this, do that, don't do this or she won't like it. Was this the way it was to be, then? To live in another woman's home, to become a kind of servant to her, was difficult enough, but to share your husband with that woman, even though that woman might be your mother-in-law! This was by far the most difficult thing. And yet she had no choice but to accept it with a smile on her face.

She locked the door behind her and went into the darkened house, took her bath as quickly as she could. When she came back into her room, only a low light burned. Her husband was asleep. She watched him for a moment. He lay under the heavy cover, his lips relaxed and almost smiling. I love him, she thought. I love him. Is it wrong to love your husband so much? Is it wrong to want him only for myself? She folded his clothing, picking it up from where he had thrown it on the mat floor, and placed it in the drawer of the chest. Then she turned out the light, crawled into her own bed beside her husband's and lay listening to his breathing. Outside, the cicada continued to sing as the city slept.

CHAPTER FOUR

THE MONTHS PASSED BY. Summer became fall, and the leaves on the maple tree in the garden turned a bright red. Sachiko tried her best to become a good wife. She strived to learn to cook rice in the way her mother-in-law wanted her to do it, even though her own mother had taught her another way. She cleaned the bath and built the fire every evening so that the family might have hot baths before bedtime. She swept the mat floors, dusted the paper sliding doors, washed the dishes, and kept the garden clean and neat. Every afternoon she took the basket and went to the vegetable market for food for the evening meal. She visited neighbors with her husband's mother, learned to listen to others talk while she smiled and spoke little. Every evening, after the evening meal was finished, she would gather up the dishes, carry them to the sink and wash them. Then she would slip into her room and sew or read, while the voices of her mother-in-law and husband floated to her through the thin walls.

Such a life was confining. Each day began and ended the same. More and more as the warm fall weather continued, she longed to escape even for a day. She would sit in the veranda, the sun streaming in upon her, and sew. The wind would bring her the scents of the garden flowers, and a hint of the city was also in the air. She looked beyond the bamboo fence of the garden and occasionally caught a glimpse of the mountains. At other times she remembered the gaiety and bustle of the streets of Tokyo, the beauty of the department stores, the quiet of a small teashop where friends could talk and listen to Western classical music.

"How I wish I could go somewhere and do something!" she cried defiantly one evening. Ichiro turned to her in surprise, then calmly went on changing his clothes. When he did not answer her, she became angry. "All I do is stay here at home. I'm nothing more than a servant. If I read too much your mother doesn't like it. She even frowns if I talk to the neighbors when I am working by the front gate. I can't make rice to please her—nothing I do seems to please her."

Almost frightened by her forwardness, she stopped. The anger drained out of her. In its place came despair, and with it a strange weakness that seized her body and held it so that she could hardly breathe. With a great effort, she turned her head from him and pretended to read the book she held in her hands, hoping that if she paid no attention the words she had said would go away.

"Sachiko!" by the tone of his voice, she knew that he had not forgotten them nor would he ever forget them. "Sachiko, you know that it's a good woman who spends her time in her home. My mother knows what is good for you. You must learn to respect her as you respected your father and brothers before you came to this house."

"My father never did insist that I be a prisoner in my own home," she cried sullenly.

"But you are no longer a part of your father's home." She had never seen his face so stern. "If your father wanted to raise you like a peasant, that was his business, but you have no right to act like one in this house. When you came into this house, you took on responsibilities to this family as well. And one of the most important of your responsibilities is not to do anything which would cause the family to lose face. Do you understand?"

"Yes, I understand," she answered, suddenly ashamed. She turned to look at him, her eyes large and serious. "I'll try to do better. I'll not complain again."

But that night, after the lights were out, she wept silently in the darkness. Fiercely she controlled herself so that her husband, who lay on his bed on the straw mat near her, could not hear the deep sobs that wrenched her body nor see the tears that poured over her cheeks. "What can I do," she cried despairingly into her hard pillow. "Is there something wrong with me that I cannot accept the role of a woman? I must learn to bear it. There is no other way."

One day a letter came for her. She had been sweeping the front walk when she heard the postman's bicycle next door. She waited, her broom in her hand, until the neighbor's door was shut and the postman appeared on the path.

"A letter for you today, *Okusama,*" he remarked from his bicycle and handed her the mail.

"A letter for me? Now who could . . ." she pondered, suddenly lighthearted. She smiled at him, struck by the realization that for the first time that day she felt like laughing or singing—anything to express the excitement of having a letter come for herself alone. She held it in her hand and stood looking down the lane after him. Soon the screech of his bicycle brakes could no longer be heard, but still she stood, a half smile on her face.

"Sachiko," her mother-in-law said to her sharply later while she sat in the veranda mending, "you've laid that sweater down several times and you haven't finished it yet. You'll have to hurry if you are to have the mending completed by dinner time."

Sachiko flushed and clutched the sweater more tightly. But her fingers could not hold the needle and her thoughts were not on her work.

For twelve days she carried the letter in her pocket. Several times she began to talk with Ichiro about it, but each time she found she could not speak. Finally, she laid it on his small study desk in their room. Then she waited until he would have time to read it.

A week went by and still he said nothing. Every day

she saw the letter in its place on his desk, but even though she knew he had read it, he did not mention it to her. She thought of it as she worked and at night she dreamed of it. The shape of the envelope, the formal black printing of the invitation—she remembered it all without even looking at it. It was written in her mind and unconsciously she recited it to herself until it became almost a song.

"Please come to the alumni class meeting to be held at the University on October 15. . . ."

That was all it said—just "Please come . . ." A little thing, she thought, but it would be so much fun. Why is it so important that I go to this meeting?

Then one evening the letter was gone. As they did every night after dinner, the soft intimate voices of her husband and mother-in-law floated from the eating room through the thin walls and into her own room. She knew that her mother-in-law held the letter, and she sat, her heart pounding and her hands clutched together in her lap, listening.

When permission was finally given, she felt strangely tired. The excitement and anticipation were gone. She made her preparations for the reunion, and when that day arrived, departed calmly, almost as if she were only going to the market. In the days following her return home again, she remembered the day as a joyful, carefree time. The friends she met and lunched with, greetings with former teachers, the freedom of being somewhere by herself and being able to make decisions by herself, the few minutes she spent with her family in her former home—all this later became the part of a beautiful dream, but a dream still tinged with unpleasantness.

"If I have to go through all that just to get permission for one day away from home," she said to herself, "it's not really worth it. I'll never ask again. It's too much trouble."

On a cold crisp morning three weeks later, Sachiko rose as usual before the rest of the family was awake.

She noticed the sky as she crouched outside the kitchen door, fanning the charcoal in the cooking brazier. The stars still shone, but in the east the sun would soon rise like a ball of fire. One by one the stars extinguished their lights, and the sun took control of the sky. "I've never seen such a beautiful sky," she said in wonder. Silently, she stood and watched. The whole earth was tinged with the golden red of the sun. A few white clouds rested in the deep blue of the sky. Even the plain wooden buildings near her glowed as if they were made of gold. "It's an omen," she breathed, almost afraid to speak. "It's an omen. My luck will change. Surely, things will become better after this!"

But all through that gloriously beautiful day, her life continued much the same as it had always been. She built a fire in the *kotatsu* under the eating table, adjusted the heavy padded blanket over the table so that the warmth might be kept under it, then prepared the *omiso* soup and set out the dried fish and sweet beans to be eaten with the rice. At each place on the table she placed slices of dried seaweed and then brought in the hot, steaming rice.

Her husband came into the room, clad in a heavy padded kimono. Little drops of water still clung to his hair and his forehead. He smiled at her and then dropped onto a cushion and stretched his legs under the blanket and down into the warmth below. Drawing the blanket around his waist, he opened the morning paper and began to read.

"Good morning, Sachiko," her mother-in-law said. Sachiko looked at her in surprise, for she was dressed in one of her loveliest kimonos. "Sachiko, I'm going to Tokyo today. You will be all right here by yourself, won't you?"

Sachiko nodded, suddenly excited at the thought of having the whole day to herself. Quickly she poured the soup and then served the rice. They ate breakfast in silence.

After her mother-in-law had left for the train station and Ichiro had departed for school, Sachiko opened the window, then carried the heavy mattresses and blankets from the house and laid them in the veranda to air. She dusted the paper doors and furniture and swept the mat floors. The morning air filled the house with a freshness and cleanliness that remained long after she had closed the windows again. The large doors facing the veranda she left open so that the sunlight might warm the house.

"Gomen kudasai!"

At first Sachiko did not hear the woman's voice from the entry of the house. Her feet thrust into wooden split-toed clogs, her hands blue from the cold water, she stood at the outdoor roofed-over sink washing clothes.

"Gomen kudasai!" This time the voice, raised slightly, carried to where Sachiko was working. She straightened, wiped her hands, and walked into the house through the kitchen, slipped off her clogs before stepping onto the mat floor and hurried to the entrance of the house.

"Kawaguchi San! Please come in."

"I've been planning to come to see you ever since the wedding, but have just been too busy. Are you in good health?"

"Yes, thank you."

"And your mother and husband?"

"They are fine, thank you. Please come in." Sachiko knelt, opened a closet and drew out a cushion. Placing it beside the table, she turned to bow formally to her guest as she stepped into the room and knelt on the mat floor. Then once more she urged, "Please sit down, and don't be afraid to make yourself comfortable." She left the room and went to the kitchen to make tea.

"Don't go to any trouble, Sachiko San. I can only stay for a short time. I'm sure you are busy."

"No, really, I am not," Sachiko answered from the kitchen. Kawaguchi San, a slender woman of about forty, wore her Western clothes well. Her skin was slightly dark, her eyes black and lively. They darted over the room, quickly evaluating each article. Her coarse, black hair, drawn back and twisted into a roll, emphasized the large bone structure of her face. When Sachiko entered the room again, Kawaguchi San's eyes were safely centered on the table, her face a polite mask, hiding the curiosity which only a moment before had been plain to see.

"I'm sorry to have kept you waiting." Sachiko placed the tray on the floor, then took the cup of hot tea from it and set it carefully before her guest. In the center of the table she placed persimmons and rice cookies.

Kawaguchi San smiled a little without parting her lips. "Your husband must be busy now. It is about time for the fall examinations, isn't it?"

"No, they were given in the first part of the month. And he is glad they are over." Sachiko peeled a persimmon, quartered and seeded it, then placed it on a small plate before the older woman. "The really busy time comes in the spring when final examinations have to be prepared." She stopped, suddenly aware that the other woman was not really listening. Her eyes looked at Sachiko strangely and once she started to speak, then fell silent again.

At last she said, "Sachiko, are you getting along all right?" Her eyes dropped to the teacup she held in her hands. Around and around she turned it—around and around until Sachiko thought she would go mad.

I must be careful, the girl thought to herself. This woman talks too much. She hesitated, then said, "Yes, I'm fine." It was said quickly—too quickly, she realized. Surely Kawaguchi San had noticed her hesitation. For just a moment Sachiko wished that she were anywhere but in this room, alone with this woman. "What right do you have to come here to pry, to question me about things that are my own private business?" She wanted to cry. She wanted to drive her from the house. She wanted to tell her never to come back again, but knew she dare not. For Kawaguchi San did have a right to be here. She had the right to know if there was trouble in the family—the right of the go-between. More than that, she was a friend of her husband's mother, a friend who would not try to keep things she heard to herself, but would do her best to let the older woman of the house know the feelings and thoughts of the younger one.

The black eyes darted back and forth, from the table to the kitchen and beyond to the outdoor sink where the clothes still waited. Kawaguchi San lowered her voice to a whisper. "Is your mother home?"

"No, she went to Tokyo this morning to visit a friend."

"She did?" Kawaguchi San licked her dry lips, then leaned across the table. "Sachiko, I really should have talked to you before you were married." She paused.

Sachiko waited, repulsed by the woman, yet forced to listen to what she had to say.

"This house, Sachiko . . ." Kawaguchi San raised her eyes and glanced fearfully around the room. "This house is haunted!"

Sachiko could hardly keep from smiling. "Oh, no!"

"Yes, it is! Ichiro San's mother knows about it. I've told her many a time that they should never have moved into a house built like this."

"But no one believes that any more, Kawaguchi San," Sachiko interrupted gravely. "That is superstition. No one believes that evil comes from the northeast, the Devil's Gate, any more."

The other woman's eyes glittered darkly. "But it does! And evil will come into this house. You wait and see!"

Calmly, Sachiko tried to reason with the woman. "But it is not built so that it faces the northeast."

"But the kitchen—that addition built on the kitchen. It protrudes in that direction!" She sat back on her heels, her face faintly triumphant.

Sachiko sat silent.

"And Ichiro San's mother—the change that has come over her within the last couple of years!" Kawaguchi San went on. "When she first moved here she was so kind and thoughtful, but now even I have trouble keeping on good terms with her. And she is one of my best friends! I feel sorry for Ichiro San," she added hastily when she saw Sachiko's shocked face. "Poor boy, it is not his fault. But no one from this community would even think of marrying him. They are sure that already the evil has entered this house." She looked at Sachiko in surprise. "Your family didn't discover it while investigating the Suzuki family?"

Sachiko shook her head wordlessly.

"I'm sorry. I should have told you and your parents." Mrs. Kawaguchi stopped, then continued thoughtfully, "Perhaps, if you were to buy charms . . ."

"We'll be all right," Sachiko said quickly. "I'm not afraid."

"If it weren't for the evil in the house," Kawaguchi San said absentmindedly, "you would be very fortunate. Ichiro San's family is a well-known one in the community where he lived before the war. His father's family were samurai, and Ichiro San has the same stature and appearance of his grandfather. You must consult a fortuneteller. That is the best thing to do, then buy a charm."

Feeling unbearably humiliated, but knowing that she must cover her feelings in order not to lose face, Sachiko forced herself to speak calmly, almost coolly. "I don't think there is anything to be concerned about, Kawaguchi San. I am very well satisfied with the arrangements, and we shall always remember your kindness to us."

"What I did was very little, but if you and Ichiro San are happy, then I am happy, too. If you do what I have told you, you should have no trouble at all." She took a sip of tea, then set it down on the table and placed the lid on the cup. "I must go. Give my regards to your mother-in-law." She knelt, her hands flat on the floor in front of her, bowed formally, then rose and moved toward the entrance. "Remember," she said as Sachiko followed her to the door, "if you need me, I will always be glad to help you."

Sachiko thanked her, walked with her to the gate. She bowed again, then watched as Kawaguchi San walked down the path toward the street. After she could see her no longer, Sachiko walked numbly back to the house. Her hands did not move as quickly as they had earlier in the morning. Her shoulders stooped a bit more than usual. She rinsed her husband's shirts and her mother-in-law's blouses, slid a bamboo pole through the sleeves and hung the garments to dry.

CHAPTER FIVE

ON A COOL LATE afternoon a few days later, Sachiko took her shopping basket and stepped down into the entry of the house.

"Sachiko, don't forget to insist that the vegetable man give you fresh carrots this time. Those yesterday were not good." At the sound of her mother-in-law's voice, Sachiko's body stiffened slightly, then she turned and stepped up again into the hallway. Across the room the old woman sat in the sun and sewed. She frowned now as she looked at the girl. "Did you buy the rice yet this month?"

"No, I haven't yet. Shall I buy it today?"

The older woman looked down at the kimono she held in her lap, pulled the needle through the material, then said impatiently, "No, no. Just remember the fish and vegetables. But you will have to hurry. Ichiro will be home soon and dinner will not be ready."

Sachiko hurried once again to the entrance. *"Ja, itte mairimasu!"*

"Itte irasshai!"

Outside the house the air was cool and crisp. The smell of fall was everywhere—in the dampness of the evening, in the golden leaves that hung from the maple trees and lay piled beneath them, in the calls of the children as they played along the street, in the ripening persimmons on the trees in the neighbor's garden. Sachiko breathed deeply and freely. Lately she had had such a feeling of depression! It was only when she could walk to the stores to shop for dinner that she was able to overcome it. She walked gracefully, her slender body poised lightly on her wooden clogs.

"Suzuki San! Where are you going? Shopping?" A laughing voice called to her from behind a tall hedge. She stopped and looked through the open gate and saw her friend Matsuoka taking clothes from bamboo poles which had hung near the veranda.

"Konnichiwa, Matsuoka San. Yes, I am. Are you going soon?"

"No, I've shopped already today. You are late, aren't you?" She tossed the clean clothes onto the polished floor of the veranda and then walked to the gate.

"I had to wait until Mother returned from town."

"Does she insist that you stay there all the time she is gone? Why don't you just get a lock for the door, and then you could be free to go any time you want."

Sachiko turned her eyes away from the direct gaze of her friend. When she did not answer, Matsuoka stirred impatiently.

"Why don't you?"

"You might be able to do something like that, but I can't," Sachiko answered at last, a little stiffly. The drums and flute of a *Chindonya* sounded from down the street. She listened to the music as it came nearer, her foot moving idly with the rhythm.

Matsuoka leaned forward, her eyes sparkling. "I know! Why don't you just slip out sometime when she's gone. No one would bother the house. Maybe the neighbors would watch it while you were gone. I haven't seen you for a long time. Remember how we used to talk before you were married? We never have any time anymore."

"The neighbors would tell her," Sachiko answered quietly. There was a short silence, broken only by the music and the running of children's feet. "You don't know how lucky you are, Matsuoka San. I wish Ichiro were not the oldest son so we could live by ourselves as you do. But of course, there is nothing I can do about it." Again the awkward silence.

Matsuoka looked down at the basket Sachiko held in

her hand. "*Maa,* I am keeping you from your work. But look! Here comes a Chindonya band. Wait and see it for just a little while, you have plenty of time, don't you?"

The light in her eyes was a challenge. Does she dominate you so much that you can't even stop to talk with a friend? they seemed to say. Do you have no will of your own? Sachiko responded to it, paused beside the road, knowing even as she did so that she would suffer if she were late.

The roadway was already crowded with children. Old men and women with babies on their backs rocked back and forth on their heels. The babies' eyes sparkled above the brightly colored blankets which tied them to their grandfathers' backs. Little girls in short skirts, their long legs bare above their stockingless *geta*-clad feet, giggled and huddled together.

She watched the Chindonya band come. There were three people. One, dressed as a woman, although anyone could tell he was a man, walked in mincing steps, his neck and face white with powder and his head heavy with an elaborate wig. Gay, old-fashioned kimonos, piercing, thumping music—they were clowns, clowns with advertising signboards on their backs.

She felt the pressure against her leg long before she thought to glance down. That was when she saw the child. It was an American child with blond, curly hair and sturdy shoulders, his mouth open now and his eyes fixed upon the disappearing Chindonya.

"Matsuoka San! Look at the beautiful child."

"Isn't he cute? He lives beside the Christian church in West Tachikawa."

The boys and girls left the side of the road and ran back to their play. Sachiko stood watching the child. She stood with the *ojiisan* and *obaasan* at the side of the road, the babies still bounced on their backs. Sachiko watched the child and thought, "Children are so much alike, no matter what color skin they have. He seems so unafraid, so self-confident!"

She saw him turn and start across the street. Then he fell, and the money he held in his hand rolled across the street and into the gutter. Shyness overcame her, overcame her concern for the child so that instead of running to help him she froze stiffly and watched as Matsuoka lifted him up and set him on his feet. They dipped his money out of the gutter, wiped it off and placed it in his hand once more. Then they stood looking after him as he self-consciously continued on his way home.

"American children are so big for their age, aren't they?" Matsuoka said thoughtfully. "He didn't want me to help him but was too polite to tell me. He must be about four, don't you think?"

Sachiko nodded absently. The evening dusk had thickened about them, and one by one lights began to come on in the houses along the street. "I really have to hurry, Matsuoka San. It's getting late, and I've got to get the shopping done and go home." She bowed. She had hardly taken a step toward the wide street beyond when she stopped short. There on the pavement lay a hundred-yen piece. The light from the street lamp was reflected in the silver of the coin.

"*Hora!* Some of the child's money on the ground." She picked it up. "What shall we do?"

"Why don't you take it to him?"

"I can't! I've got to get home right away. Besides, I don't know where he lives. Matsuoka San, please return it to him!"

"All right. I will. My husband doesn't get home until seven, and so I have plenty of time."

"Well, good-by, then."

"*Sayonara!*"

The vegetable market was crowded with women shoppers when Sachiko finally reached the main street. She stood at one side of the open shop, waiting her turn, but wishing she had the courage to push ahead as some of the women did. Again at the fish market she had to wait until the fish she chose were cleaned and wrapped. Then, uneasily, almost with panic, she hurried back along the darkened side streets, between the hedges on either side, to her home.

The light above the entrance door was on when she approached the house. Her steps faltered. She stopped in the shadows of a tall pine tree that twisted its way over the top of the gate.

I'm late again, she thought frantically. After what happened last time, I can't go through it again! The light from the eating room streamed into the garden, but the rest of the house was dark. She's in there talking about me and he'll believe anything she says. Sachiko shivered and clutched her sweater more closely about her. It's such a little thing—to be late! But she'll twist it into something far more important than it is. She grasped the basket more tightly in her hand and took several steps toward the entrance. "I have to go in," she told herself aloud, but even as she said it, she paused, then returned to the safe darkness. She set the basket down, and her hand found the rough bark of the tree.

Night sounds pressed themselves upon her—night sounds and the smell of chrysanthemums, cooked vegetables and fish, the rich damp odor of the earth in the garden. An airplane roared overhead. She followed the lights with her eyes until it disappeared. But even in the silence which it left behind, she heard the tiny rustlings of the earth dwellers. A cricket. A bird in the top of the tree. A cat slipping by on soft cushioned feet.

She remembered Matsuoka's laughing, frank gaze. The teasing voice seemed to float on the damp air. "Why don't you just get a lock on the door . . . slip out when she's gone . . . come and see me sometime . . . you never come . . . I have plenty of time."

The year she was seven she had lain awake in her bed on the mat floor waiting for morning to come—the morning of the Shichi-go-san Festival. Near her, folded neatly and ready for the next day, lay her kimono, *haori* jacket, white stocking *tabi,* and large bowed hair ribbon. But most wonderful of all was the new white and red obi tie, the first she had ever had. When morning came, she lay waiting until her mother opened the heavy wood shutters. The sun streamed across the mat floor, caught the golden threads in the obi, and whirled them up into the sunbeams that danced on the veranda.

"Mother, may I put on my kimono now?" she asked at once. Her mother smiled and said, "Sachiko, we must wait until we have eaten and until the house is cleaned." So she had touched them gently and then dressed in her school clothes.

The morning had seemed very long to her. She waited until the smell of *omiso* soup and fish filled the air. Mixed with it was the richly sweet odor of incense. Grandmother was offering the first foods of the day to the ancestors.

"Sachiko, you must eat. Today will be a busy one for you," her mother told her when she ate a bite of rice and then set the bowl and chopsticks down again.

She smiled up at her mother. "It's so much fun, isn't it, Mother? And I'm glad you are going with me to the shrine."

Her mother smiled back. "I'm glad, too."

But her mother had not gone. Her grandmother had announced suddenly that she had decided to go.

"Won't Mother go?" Sachiko had said apprehensively, laying aside all pretense of eating.

"Someone has to stay in the house. It's not safe to leave it unattended."

"But I want Mother to go!" Sachiko had kicked and cried. When she saw the white, frozen look on her mother's face she had begun to scream loudly, partly to get her own way and partly because she was frightened. Soon afterward she found herself dressed with the red ribbon in her hair and her feet clad in the white *tabi* and high-platform *zori* sandals. The house was quiet when she left with her grandmother, but from far back in the house came the sound of sobs, muffled and indistinct.

On another day, as she watched her mother iron, she had asked curiously, "Mother, why does the clothing become so smooth when you iron?" Her mother had replied, "Anything that is warmed first has a tendency to become smooth." Strangely, she was reminded of the day of the Shichi-go-san Festival. Childlike, she translated the meaning to her own understanding—"Not everything that is warmed or kindly treated becomes smooth and loving." From that day she ceased to look at adults as a child does. Something caused her to be not quite so willing to trust. She discovered that the world of grown-ups was not always as free as it seemed.

Then she knew, standing in the darkness of the garden, that her life must be as her mother's had been while her grandmother had lived—a life of trying desperately to warm so that things might become smooth. Trying to forget herself in order to find peace. Trying not to be noticed so that some part of her might belong to herself. She realized dully that what her mother had taught must be true. Before marriage a good woman owes her respect to her father and brothers—after marriage to her mother-in-law and husband.

Picking up the basket she turned away from the brightness of the front entrance onto a small path which led past the storehouse and doghouse. She opened the side door and stepped into the kitchen, turning on the light switch as she walked by. The room was cold and plainly furnished—a bright new gas hot plate, open cupboards which held pots and pans and dishes, a cutting board.

The voices of Ichiro and his mother drifted to her from the eating room, but she paid little attention to them now. "He's home already! I must hurry!" She measured the rice, then carried it to the sink and washed it time after time until the water became clear.

Then, lighting the fire, she set the rice pot on it and covered the pan with a lid. Her hands were cold and stiff, but she worked quickly, preparing the vegetables and soup. Then she placed the relishes carefully on individual dishes.

"Sachiko!" She started nervously when she heard her husband's voice.

"*Hai!*" Placing the relishes on the tray, she pushed open the door which led to the eating room. After she stepped up into the room, she knelt, placed the tray on the floor and closed the door again. When she turned to look at her husband, she knew that for the first time he was really angry with her. She avoided her mother-in-law's eyes and remained where she was, her own eyes on the floor.

"What are you doing—taking so long to get dinner? Don't you know I'm hungry?"

She sat there numbly. There was nothing to say.

"You know I want you here at home when I get back from school. Where were you?"

"She went shopping, Ichiro," his mother answered. "I asked her to get a few things for dinner."

"But surely it doesn't take an hour to go shopping!"

"The market was crowded," Sachiko said, her face flushing.

Her mother-in-law turned deliberately toward her. "You met a friend of yours, didn't you, Sachiko?"

She did not answer. She was seized suddenly with an intense anger. It flooded her whole body, held her as one possessed by devils. I hate her! she thought. I hate her for spying on me—for pretending to be sympathetic. She shuddered slightly, but her face remained inscrutable.

"Well, don't just sit there! Let's eat!"

She felt the weight of his gaze as, trembling, she placed the dishes on the table and fled to the kitchen. There, her body pressed against the door, she listened unashamedly.

"You know," she heard her mother-in-law say, "I've been thinking about Sachiko. I wonder if we made a mistake about her."

"Sachiko tries, Mother. I'm sure she does."

"Yes, but when I think of how different she has turned out to be from what we thought she was . . . I don't blame Kawaguchi San. I don't think it is her fault. But the girl's family must have hidden her real character from us." The poison was at work again!

"Mother, Sachiko is a good wife. She'll learn with more experience," Ichiro repeated wearily, almost with irritation.

"I wonder why the investigations didn't bring it out," she continued softly as if she were unaware he had spoken.

"Well, it's over now. The wedding is over."

"You know, the daughter of that teacher—that friend of Tanada Sensei; she might have fitted better. But then," she paused, "no one knows. We might have had trouble with her, too. I tell you, Ichiro," her voice rose, "it's difficult these days to find very many young girls who are suitable for marriage. I've no use for these modern girls!"

"I don't think Sachiko is modern, Mother. Her family is an old one. Her father is respected. Kawaguchi San told us that."

"Somewhere, somehow, she has been badly trained, then. I try to teach her, but she always seems to do everything wrong. If she hadn't graduated from a university, I would have thought that she was not teachable." Plaintively she continued, "It's not easy, Ichiro—training a young girl. I try my best, but it is terribly hard to get her to do things the way she should."

"I understand, Mother. You've worked hard for me all your life, and I'll always appreciate it. I'll never forget how difficult it was for you after the war, taking care of the shop so that I could go to school. You need to rest now and not work so hard."

"It wasn't easy," she admitted slowly, remembering. "The humiliation of having to forget the samurai heritage of this family and to open a shop . . ." A long pause. "To think that before your father died, I had maids to do my work and a large house in Tokyo. But that is all over now."

In the kitchen the gas flame sputtered. Sachiko sat crouched against the door for a moment longer. Then straightening her apron and flexing her stiff legs, she stood and turned off the fire under the rice pot. It sputtered several times, casting a blue reflection over her pale face. Then the flame went out. The room became uncomfortably quiet.

"I'll talk to Sachiko," came her young husband's voice from the next room. "I'll talk to her tonight."

CHAPTER SIX

"SACHIKO SAN!"

Sachiko finished throwing the mattresses over the bamboo poles, then looked toward the gate. Matsuoka stood just outside the garden on the path, beckoning to her. Glancing swiftly into the house, she saw her mother-in-law still at work on the new kimono.

"Matsuoka San, I can't talk very long. I was late getting home last night and had a terrible time."

"Can't we talk some other time? I've got something I want to tell you."

"Why don't you come this afternoon. *Okaasan* is going to be gone for a while. Come after two," she whispered, her eyes still fixed on the front door.

"*Hai*. I'll come." Matsuoka slipped down the path toward the street.

I hate to scheme and lie to do the things I want, Sachiko thought as she walked slowly back to the veranda where the rest of the mattresses lay waiting to be aired. And yet, she continued to herself, if Ichiro's mother knew I was making plans to see friends, she would think I was deliberately trying to disobey her. Can I help it? She seems to find something wrong with almost everything I do. Her eyes stared blankly at the dying chrysanthemums in the garden. If I can't love her, at least I'll have to learn to respect her. But it is hard to do even that! She thought of her husband who was torn between a dawning affection for her and the desire to be obedient to his mother—Ichiro, with the engaging cleft in his chin, the broad shoulders, and eyes that might someday hold love for her.

"Perhaps he loves me already," she said to herself

dreamily. "Perhaps he does and is unable to tell me." Her eyes began to shine, and lifting her head she looked out into the garden. She felt the autumn sun warm on her face. Its rays came through the branches of the bamboo tree, still lushly green from the fall rains.

"The bamboo tree," she said to herself thoughtfully. "The bamboo tree always bends, but never breaks—never tries to go against the wind and the rain. If I could be like that tree! Never rebelling, always swaying, surrendering, bending with the wind so that in the end, after the storm is over, it can spring up stronger than ever."

She sat on the veranda, almost dazed by her thoughts. Murmuring to herself, she registered her decision: "I, too, must bend! I must give! But I won't break! If I must surrender a small part of myself to gain my husband and to keep peace in this family, I will do it." Some of the joy in her flowed out into the brightness of the morning.

She had just set the cakes on a tray when she heard Matsuoka at the entrance.

"Sachiko San!"

"Matsuoka San? Come in." She slipped a clean apron over her skirt and sweater and hurried to the door. "I'm so glad you could come. Come in," she said again.

Matsuoka stepped out of the entrance, slowly drew off her gloves. "Don't bother about tea. A friend of my mother stopped by just an hour ago, and I drank so much I just can't drink any more." She stopped, then pleaded, "May I see your trousseau? I've wanted to see it for such a long time!"

"Of course," Sachiko laughed as she led the other girl to the corner room. "I really don't have a great deal, but you are welcome to look all you wish."

"Your father gave you the chest? It's lovely!" She watched as Sachiko opened a sliding door and drew out the colorful mattresses. "Oh, what beautiful *futon!* Sachiko San," she said warmly, her eyes sparkling, "you are such a wonderful person! You shouldn't have any difficulty making people care for you."

Sachiko smiled. "Believe it or not, I have quite a bit of difficulty sometimes."

"Oh, your mother-in-law!" Matsuoka shrugged. "Anyone is bound to have a certain amount of trouble at first with one's mother-in-law, especially if you have to live with her. I'm fortunate I don't have to live with mine. If I did, I would certainly have problems!" She paused, then continued swiftly, "But certainly, she's getting used to you by now!"

Sachiko's smile faded. "She hates me," she said indistinctly.

"Oh, surely, it's not as bad as that!"

"Yes, she does. I've tried every way I can to please her, but she's never satisfied. Do you know what I think?" Her eyes gazed seriously at Matsuoka. "I think she's jealous! Isn't that silly? Jealous of me!"

They sat in silence for a while, trying to match the things they had unconsciously felt or seen with the words which had just been said.

"What about your husband?" Matsuoka said at last.

Sachiko did not answer her. She sat sunk in her own thoughts, gazing out the window. The cry of the vegetable man came to them, but they were hardly aware that he had called. Soon he passed on down the street, his voice fading as he turned the corner.

"Sachiko San, what does he think?"

"I don't know."

"You don't know?"

"Well—I don't know for sure. I only know what I think."

"What do you think?" her friend prodded.

Sachiko felt a flush mount from the base of her throat and spread across her face. "I think that if she would let him, he would love me."

"Love! You mean you believe in love?" Matsuoka

laughed openly, mockingly. Confused and embarrassed, Sachiko lowered her eyes. Matsuoka stopped laughing, but her eyes still sparkled. "Sachiko San! You don't marry for love! You marry because you want a home—or to keep from disgracing your parents! Do you think he married you because he loved you?" she went on, irony in her tones. "Your husband married you because his mother thought you would be easily guided and trained into doing the housework she didn't want to do. He married you because he wanted someone to wash his clothes, get his slippers ready for him when he returns at night, and because he wants someone to bear his children and prepare his food."

"But Matsuoka San! My father told me that many times people learn to love after they are married awhile."

"You have been seeing too many American movies!"

"No, really, it's not that at all. It is love when you care for each other, isn't it? And because a woman learns to care for her husband, she wants to do something for him. She wants to wash his clothes and do ordinary things that will show him she cares for him." She paused, then continued slowly, "She wants to bear his children." She was silent for a moment then said intensely, "You sound so bitter!"

"No, I'm not bitter," Matsuoka responded gently. "I guess I want to think the same way you do about it." She laughed ruefully. "It's strange, isn't it—how you are the one who is so traditional in so many ways. And yet you have surprisingly modern ideas, while I, who consider myself somewhat modern, am not quite so free in my thoughts as you are about some things. I can see how you would probably run into trouble with a mother-in-law such as you have." She glanced at Sachiko curiously. "She doesn't know how you feel, does she?"

"Of course not! I don't talk to her!"

"But your husband does, doesn't he?"

Sachiko sat in silence for a moment. Then, ignoring the question, she said lightly, "Let's go into the other room. We can talk in there much easier."

"Sachiko San, I'm sorry. I wasn't too tactful, was I?" Matsuoka was conscious, suddenly, of having said too much.

"No, really," Sachiko said slowly and rose to her feet. "It's true. I just haven't wanted to accept it." She fingered a book on the desk absentmindedly. "I've tried to tell myself that every wife has that problem."

"Does it happen every night—their talking together, I mean?" Matsuoka couldn't resist asking.

"Yes."

"And you don't stay to talk with them?"

"I've never felt that I'm wanted."

"Well, it's not typical of every wife! Sachiko San, it's really not!" Matsuoka's face flushed indignantly. "It's not fair. I wouldn't stand for it."

"Maa, Matsuoka San!" Sachiko laughed but there was a sob in her throat. "You certainly express yourself freely."

The other girl's face became suddenly still. "I know I do, and it has caused me plenty of problems." Her voice was subdued, but it didn't remain that way long. "You know," she continued swiftly, "you can still find places in the country where people are as old-fashioned as your mother-in-law, but it's unusual to find much of it in the city anymore."

"Mother had trouble until Grandmother died."

"Yes, but that was—how many years ago?"

"Yes, I know. But you still hear of it once in a while even yet." Sachiko walked to the door. "Come, let's go into the other room," she urged, and led the way through the small hall to the eating room.

When her guest was seated before the table, she handed her a large, decorated photograph album. "Here, this is something I've wanted you to see. While you look at it, I'll bring tea."

Matsuoka opened the book. She looked not at the beginning of it where she knew she would find pictures of Sachiko's childhood, but instead turned to the end of the book and found there that for which she was seeking—a picture of a serious young man dressed in formal black evening clothes with his equally serious bride. The large white head covering and black traditional kimono with elaborate designs only served to make Sachiko's small face seem smaller and paler than it usually was.

"Sachiko San," Matsuoka said as she watched her friend place the cake and tea on the table before them, "do you remember the child yesterday who dropped his money after we watched the Chindonya?"

"The American child?"

"Yes."

"I remember. Did you take the money back?"

"Yes. That was what I wanted to tell you about. It was really an interesting experience." Matsuoka moved her legs to one side of the cushion and settled herself more comfortably. "I went to the church first and asked, because I wasn't sure just where the child lived. The teacher there sent me to a Western-style house next to the church. The child's mother came to the door, and I became so nervous that I couldn't think of anything to say in English but good morning, and I knew that wasn't right. So I didn't say anything. But when she spoke I was so relieved, for she spoke Japanese! We talked for a long time in the entrance, and then she told me about this class!"

She paused thoughtfully, turning the cup around in her hands. Then setting the cup down in the small plate before her, she continued, "It's a class to learn American cooking, Sachiko San!" Excitement shone in her eyes and on her face. "Wouldn't you like to learn to cook American food? Think how we could impress our husbands! You know most men love American food!"

"It sounds interesting," Sachiko agreed.

"Do you think you could go?" the other girl continued eagerly. "It meets only once a month and costs scarcely anything at all! Ask your husband if you can go!"

"I would really like to go, but I've never been in a Western house. I wouldn't know how to act."

"I wouldn't worry about that. No one else will know what to do, either, so no one will be watching us particularly."

"I'd really like to go," Sachiko repeated, a note of hope in her voice. "Is that all they do—study cooking?"

"Oh, she said they sing, too. And study Christianity a little. Even that might be interesting. Anyway, it would be fun to go somewhere and do something, wouldn't it?"

"Yes, it would be fun!" Do I dare risk more criticism by asking to go? Sachiko wondered. Certainly she wouldn't care if I were gone only one afternoon a month. "Do I dare?" she echoed aloud.

"Please ask him, Sachiko San!" Matsuoka's eyes darkened with the intensity of her feelings. "Don't let her dominate you! She can only hurt you as much as you let her. Don't let her do it!"

"Yes, but she's not your mother-in-law. You don't have to live with her when she's angry!"

"I know. That is true, but I hate to see you change into a person with no will and personality of your own. You can be respectful and still belong to yourself!"

"I hope so, Matsuoka San. But I will ask him," she decided suddenly. "I'll ask him if I can go and if he says I can, I'll let you know. Is that all right?"

"Yes, of course. But I hope you can go. It would be so much more fun if we could go together."

"I'll ask him."

She waited until the house was quiet that night before

she approached her husband. She waited until he was fed, had had his bath, was happy and comfortable before she mentioned the class. Then she stood waiting, her heart pounding as she watched his face for his answer. At first she thought it was to be no. She saw him frown and knew that he had not wanted to be disturbed. But then his face became smooth and noncommittal again.

"We'll see," he answered finally. "Let me think about it for a couple of days." He turned back to his desk and began correcting papers his students had written, his brow furrowed and his eyes intent.

He is angry that I would disturb him—not just about the class, but about anything, she thought. He doesn't like to be caught in the role of go-between. But in what other way could I manage to reach his mother? Acutely distressed at having had to upset her husband, Sachiko walked out of the room and into the garden.

A noise startled her and she stood silently for a moment until her eyes could become adjusted to the night. A thumping noise came from the storehouse. "Shiro!" She laughed and ran into the darkness of the storehouse, picked up the wiggling soft body of Ichiro's dog. He struggled, deliriously happy at her attention. Before he became quiet, she had hair in her mouth and his wet kisses on her face. "What a rascal! Have you been lonesome?" His tail thumped yes and once again she dodged his tongue. They laughed together softly in the night—the dog and the girl—sharing a secret joke and enjoying it. Understanding each other. Shutting out any who did not understand that a person and a dog could talk to each other—especially if the human was young and soft and had a voice that laughed.

Ichiro came into their room the next evening, and suddenly she knew by the sparkle in his eyes what the answer was to be. He had received permission for her to go to the cooking class! Satisfied, feeling slightly triumphant, she turned back to the dressing table and continued brushing her hair. She smiled, thinking of the fun she would have; then, the brushing finished, still smiling she began to comb her hair. Suddenly her hand stopped in midair and she turned to see him sitting on the edge of the *futon* watching her.

"Come here," he commanded, and his eyes laughed and teased her.

She paused for a moment, coquettishly testing him. When he reached for her, she eluded him, laughing softly. He caught her, thrust his face against the soft skin of her neck, felt the warmth that was part of her. She struggled, weak from laughter.

"Be still!" He held her tightly, strongly. "Be still, or I'll beat you!" Again, uncontrollably shaken with giggles, she looked at him, and he began to laugh with her.

Then she stopped laughing, suddenly aware of his face close to hers, his arms holding her body firmly against his. He moved so that her head rested against the hollow of his shoulder where she could hear his heart beating. Their laughter quieted, they listened to the stillness of the night.

"It'll work out." Softly he spoke of the anxiety that had been in their minds through the preceding weeks. Without asking, she knew what he meant. She let her body melt against his—let it speak for her words that were difficult for her lips. His arms tightened about her. "My parents were very close," he remembered, thinking of the warmth of his mother's face in the days preceding his father's death. "We'll be all right."

"My father says that love comes after marriage in Japan," she murmured. Then, afraid lest she had been too bold, she shrank back against him.

A long pause. Too long? she wondered. Had she said what she should not have said? Had she ruined all chances of anything really warm and strong developing between them? Sick at heart, her body suddenly drained of emotion, she waited, hope hanging on his answer.

Thoughtfully, ponderingly, he weighed the words. "Love? Is it possible?" Then his lips brushed the top of her head, fleetingly touched her hair, and she felt his breath against her face once more. "Possible? Time will bring the answer." How difficult to use words! They failed one so often!

Then words came to him. "Love? Yes, of course. If you feel as I do, then love it truly is." His face suddenly alight, he turned her toward him.

In the dimness of the lamp light she saw the light in his eyes deepen. She thrust her arms around him and held him. She knew that, though they might not put it into words, what they felt was love.

CHAPTER SEVEN

"THERE'S THE CHURCH," Matsuoka said to Sachiko as they turned onto a narrow road from a broader thoroughfare in the western part of the city. "You can just see the top of the steeple and the cross from here, but it isn't far."

"Does the American woman live near the church?"

"Yes. They are missionaries."

They walked down the narrow paved street, crossed a railroad track, and continued walking. The road was bordered by a line of houses, broken occasionally by a farmer's field. The closer they drew to the church and the larger grew the steeple and the cross that overlooked the community, the slower Sachiko walked. Finally, she stopped short, her heart pounding.

"Matsuoka San, I just can't go."

"What's the matter? Have you forgotten something?"

Sachiko flushed. "No." She searched desperately for some reason she could give for having to return home, but could think of nothing but that she was suddenly, unreasonably frightened. "I've never gone to an American's home," she gasped. "I wouldn't know how to act."

"Sachiko San, it's all right. Really, there is nothing to be worried about," her friend reassured her. "Are you afraid of the Americans?"

"No, of course not!"

"I should hope you aren't. If anyone were to see you now he would think you had never seen an American! He would think you were from the country!"

"I said I'm not afraid of the woman!" Sachiko became so irritated that she forgot her fright. Matsuoka laughed when she saw that she had succeeded in calming her. Sachiko smiled reluctantly. "I was silly, wasn't I?"

"Yes, you were. It was rather a surprising thing to hear from a girl as well educated as you are."

"It's not even going to an American's house that scares me. I think it is that I have been almost nowhere since I've been married. I've forgotten how to act!" She started walking again, all the while looking about her quickly to see if anyone had noticed them.

"You'll be all right. You won't have to talk. No one minds if a young girl doesn't say very much. The older women will want to do all the talking anyway." Matsuoka giggled suddenly. "I'll have to be still, too, and that will be pretty hard for me!"

They were still laughing when they rounded the curve of the road.

The church was of wood, painted white. Its lines were simple. The yard was trampled smooth by the feet of children who played there every day, and one of its windows still bore a hole made by a child's baseball. A group of swings, a set of ladders, a slide, chinning bars, and a tree that swung slightly sideways from the weight of the many little boys who had paused to hang from a convenient limb on their climb to the topmost branches —they all told the story of loving wear and use. When Sachiko and Matsuoka approached the church, they saw lines upon lines of children dressed in uniforms of blue, waiting for their teacher to take them safely home from a morning in kindergarten.

Beside the church sat the missionary's house. It was enclosed by a stained-wood picket fence, and the grass on the lawn was still green from the fall rainy season. Two pines lined the straight path to the door and chrysanthemums bloomed in profusion beside the fence.

They rang the bell and waited. Through the screen they could see that the *genkan* was full of shoes left by their owners in straight rows. Here and there was a pair of wooden *geta* or women's plastic *zori* with velvet straps.

The door opened and for just a moment Sachiko was aware of the warmth in the missionary's smile; then the girls stepped out of their *zori* and up onto the polished wood floor. Soon she and Matsuoka found themselves seated near the doorway of a Japanese-style mat-floor room.

The room was bare of furniture except for a small pump organ that sat against the wall. Large flat cushions lay in a circle on the *tatami* floor, and a simple flower arrangement stood in the alcove before a hanging picture. The paper doors which guarded the entrance to the veranda were open. The afternoon sun poured into the room, warming it so that the guests sat as far back out of the sunshine as they could. Children in the kindergarten playground outside the garden called to each other, and now and then the cry of a baby came from a nearby house. It was a lazy warm afternoon—a fly buzzed outside the veranda, and the smell of late fall was thick in the air.

The woman next to Sachiko was talking constantly to another woman across the room. She was heavy-set and middle-aged, clad in a dark kimono. Her face perspired slightly from the warmth of the room, and every few minutes she would draw a paper handkerchief from the sleeve of her kimono and wipe her forehead carefully.

"I thought I wouldn't be able to come today," she was saying. "I had to get the *futon* aired, and just before I was ready to leave, a guest came. But he didn't stay long and so I arrived on time."

"Did Mitsugi San come?"

"No. She had to attend PTA at the primary school today. The women from Gochi aren't here today." Out came the paper handkerchief.

Sachiko turned her eyes toward the garden, but not before she caught the very slight glimmer of laughter in Matsuoka's eyes. Smothering a giggle, Sachiko concentrated on a butterfly that had lighted on the veranda, watched it chase itself across the polished floor and finally flutter away. Then the sliding door opened, and the missionary came into the room.

Sachiko watched her as she talked to the perspiring woman. Her eyes were large and clear in the slenderness of her face. It was a quiet face, but there was a strange intensity about her that drew Sachiko and fascinated her. Her dark brown hair was streaked with strands of gold which, when seen in the sunlight, seemed almost red. Her face did not look as young as Sachiko had first thought. There were laugh wrinkles in the corners of her eyes and mouth, but her skin was clear and unblemished. When she stood to walk to the organ, she walked gracefully, but slightly self-consciously, bent over slightly when passing before the women seated on the floor.

What is she like? wondered Sachiko. She thought of the missionary teachers she had in her classes at the university. They were usually older, unmarried women, and she had never felt particularly close to them. Suddenly she felt an intense desire to know all she could about this missionary—what she did every day, what she thought, the kind of relationship she had with her husband and child. When the other women sang the hymns Sachiko sat with her eyes fixed unseeingly on the open hymnal, her head whirling and dancing with new thoughts, but her face composed and polite. She was faintly aware of Matsuoka singing beside her and recognized the tune as one she had sung with some friends at the university. "What a friend we have in Jesus . . ." but the words had no meaning for her. She sang because she knew the song and not because she understood it.

She watched the women, wondered about them—wondered why they had come, what they felt and thought about the American religion. "Which ones are believers in Christianity?" she asked herself. "Why should they leave the religion of their own people to accept a foreign religion?" The woman next to her must be a Christian, for the missionary woman asked her to pray. Perhaps the one to whom she had been talking was also a Christian. One of the women was younger than the others and one was an old woman, a grandmother with bent shoulders and gray hair. The woman next to the grandmother carried a baby on her back. The baby whimpered and the mother's body swayed slightly. The baby slept again. The fly buzzed . . . and the missionary's slightly foreign accent, though easily understood, fell strangely on their ears.

"Some people think that Christianity is hard to understand, but instead, it is so simple that even a child can become a Christian. Jesus came into the world to tell of God's love for us. He loved us so much that he was willing to die for us in order that we might know him as our friend. A Christian is one who has accepted this friendship Christ offers us.

"We cannot understand why God loves us, for we are not lovely people. He knows that we have done wrong, and yet he loves us. We do not understand many things; yet he loves us. When we think of this, we know that we, too, must love those who are not easy to love. We must love those who are not beautiful or rich—those who do not wear fine clothes. We know that we, too must love those who do not love us, just as Jesus did."

Sachiko watched the woman's face, not quite understanding what she was saying, but somehow touched by the warmth of it—the positive joy of it striking a response within her. The missionary's warm smile appeared often as she talked. Even when her lips failed to smile, somehow her eyes seemed to smile.

"The whole message of Christianity is based on love. It is a message of God's love for us. It is this love which God has given us that helps us to be kind to others. Without this love, we could not love our enemies. But because God has loved us, he has made it possible for us to love even those who want to harm us.

"When we become Christians, our hearts are changed. We then teach our children to be kind because Jesus told us to be kind. We love our neighbor even though that neighbor may not love us. We become better and more understanding wives and mothers because we have love for God and others in our hearts. We serve God in all we do, whether it be working in our homes, playing with our children, talking and working with our neighbors. We do this because we have love in our hearts and because our Friend, Jesus Christ, lives in our hearts."

Although she did not understand the meaning of the words that were spoken that day, Sachiko thought often about them. And she thought of the feelings she had had the day she had gone only to learn American cooking and had heard so many other things which filled her with wonderings and questions. Is the American god like Jizo Sama who guards and protects children? Or is he another god to add to the many other gods we worship? She remembered seeing in a friend's home a picture of Jesus placed on the family Shinto god-shelf. Was this what the missionary expected them to do?

She also remembered how light and joyful the Christian women had looked on that day when they told how they had accepted the belief of the Christians. She remembered the happy, restful feeling she had had as she listened to them. It can't be bad, she thought, for it made me feel so good. The smile on the face of the missionary, the quiet of the afternoon, the simplicity of the music—they held none of the darkness and heavy ritual of the Buddhist temples.

The women had laughed afterward. They had laughed and talked as they watched the missionary make a cake, all the while examining the kitchen covertly—the painted walls, the cabinets, the stove and the refrigerator. Laughing and working together they had felt a strange closeness to each other.

"I want to go again," Sachiko said to Matsuoka as

they made their way down the street toward the bus stop. "I really enjoyed it so much."

"I did, too. We'll go next month."

"Yes, I want to go every time I possibly can."

So every month Sachiko went with Matsuoka to the missionary's house. Every month she learned to sing a little more, to smile often, to be not quite so afraid to speak. One month she bought a Bible and from that time, while her husband and mother-in-law talked every evening after dinner, she read, stopping now and then to think about the new ideas she was learning. Some days she sang as she washed. She smiled and her husband returned the smiles. In the blindness of her new-found satisfaction and joy, she thought that everyone was as happy as she. She forgot her mother-in-law except at times when she had to try especially hard to obey her. But even at such times she often only felt sorry for her husband's mother.

Sachiko could see the sharp, speculative glances the older woman sent her, particularly when she returned to her work with a smile on her face after talking with her husband, or when she failed to become angry at some unreasonable task her mother-in-law gave her to perform. Soon, Ichiro began to leave the table early. More and more often, the laughter and conversation echoed now from the corner room belonging to the young couple.

When this happened, the older woman, alone in her own room, pursed her lips and reached again for the ever-present kimono. The nights were long, and she could not sleep, so she sewed—and waited. With the tenacity and patience of the old, she waited. Time would work in her favor. She was willing to sit by herself until it did.

CHAPTER EIGHT

TWO YEARS PASSED and again winter was upon them. The cold wind crept into the kitchen from the north and tried to invade the rest of the house. Sachiko still smiled and sang, but her singing was quieter and she was not so innocently unaware of her mother-in-law's feelings as she had been before. When the sun shone in the morning and the heavy wooden shutters were opened wide to the morning air, the house seemed larger and the two women felt not quite so aware of each other's faults nor of their disagreements.

But when the damp of the evening spread into the garden, and the *futon* were taken quickly from the horizontally hung poles and laid in the closets, when the heavy *amado* were shut again—then they became acutely aware that there were two mistresses in the house. The house seemed divided and torn in two with the unsaid words and feelings that ravaged it. The darkness, the *amado,* the necessity of guarding their words while the man was in the house, the cold which forced them to spend most of their time together in the intimacy of the *kotatsu,* their feet stuck down into the hole in the floor where the brazier blazed under the heavy blanket which bound them warmly together—all these were bitter reminders of the antagonisms that lay between the two women. What should have been a unifying experience became a time for silence—uncomfortable silence on the part of the young wife, and bitter, critical silence from the older woman.

Sachiko washed and cleaned, rose at dawn every morning, long before her husband and mother-in-law were awake, to make the breakfast and build the fire in the *kotatsu.* She stayed up after the rest of the family had gone to bed, bathed in water used first by her husband and then her husband's mother, and finished the work that had not yet been completed that day. Her fragile face grew thinner but more beautiful, and the dignity that grew in her did not match the red soreness of her hands caused by countless days of washing clothes and dishes in cold water in the open outdoor sink. She complained less often, but snatched more and more time in the evening to read from the Bible she had bought two years before and which was now faded and worn from use.

Yoshiko Suzuki, too, had grown thinner, and sometimes when she moved about the house she would stop suddenly with a look of surprise on her face as she waited for the pain that had come to live in her body to fade away. The skin on her face had drawn tighter until her mouth was a thin, narrow line which curved rarely into a smile. Her eyes were hard, especially when they looked upon her daughter-in-law. It was not often that her face softened. When it did, it was because she was thinking of her son and of what he must accomplish.

New Year's Eve came. Sachiko sat with her feet in the *kotatsu,* waiting for her husband and mother-in-law to come home from their visit to the Buddhist temple. The night was dark, but clear and cold. It was so still in the house that the ticking of the clock on the wall sounded loud in the quietness of the room. Now and then she would put down the needle and the clothes she was mending and rub her back. Sometimes she would doze so that her head almost touched the table over the *kotatsu* and her needle would become lost in the folds of the quilt that covered the table and kept the heat warm about her feet and legs.

"I'm so tired," she cried one time after she had again lost the needle and had to climb out of the *kotatsu* to look for it. If it were in the *kotatsu* pit, she would never find it that evening! "I've got to find it! If I lose many more needles, she will say that I am wasteful and will be angry again," she fretted aloud. But it was gone, and although she looked again and again, she was not able to find it. "It's slipped down between the *tatami* mats," she told herself, "and I'm not going to take them up again!" She laughed almost hysterically, remembering the hours that week she had spent taking out the heavy six-foot-long mats, cleaning them outdoors, and then fitting them back together like a jig-saw puzzle into each of the rooms. She folded the clothes she had not yet finished and took them into her room. Then, opening the closet doors, she pushed them as far back into the closet as possible so that they might not be seen during the coming New Year's holidays.

Sachiko stood for a moment and looked about the room. It was spotlessly clean, as were all the other rooms. That week she had cleaned the house completely, replaced the paper in the *shoji* doors with clean white paper, repaired the holiday kimonos, prepared a special flower arrangement for the *tokonoma* of the guest room. The garden was swept and the doorway outside decorated with a special New Year's decoration of pine, bamboo, rice cake, and oranges. She had shopped and cooked so that the food for the coming week of holidays was prepared—special sweet bean soup for her husband and plenty of rice cakes to toast over the brazier. In the kitchen were containers full of rice cookies and candy. Beside them stood several bottles of sake. Even though Ichiro did not drink, guests who would come to see them would expect to have it, she thought as she went back into he room.

Tossing aside the quilt that covered the table over the *kotatsu,* she looked down into the brazier. The coals were still hot and red, and as she watched, a tongue of flame reached up hungrily toward the screen that covered them, then sank back into the bed of hot charcoal that fed it. It will be all right, she decided. They won't be gone more than an hour and a half, and it will still be hot when they return. Then, placing the quilt carefully over the mat floor around the hole, she went to the door and into the hallway which led to the bathroom. There she stepped into wooden clogs and opened the top of the wooden bathtub. The water was still hot; the room also felt warm from the fire that burned in the little stove in the tub. She closed the lid quickly so the room would not become full of steam and went back into the eating room. Her work was done. There was nothing more for her to do but wait.

She dozed again, the warmth of the *kotatsu* making her sleepy. Then, so quietly that she hardly heard them at first, came the sound of the *Joya no kane,* the watch-night bells of the temple. Motionless she sat, the deep, slow, ponderous ringing seemingly entering into her very bones. Her eyes remained closed, but she no longer slept. The old year with its pain, its mistakes, its bitter, hard work was over. It would never come again. Again and again the bells sounded. Over all the land of Japan the bells from the temples were ringing, telling of the passing of the old year. With the solemn chiming of each bell, people hoped for deliverance from their sins. One hundred and eight times it would ring.

"Cleanse me of hatred!" someone somewhere would be crying as she counted the bells. "Cleanse me of jealousy!" "Cleanse me of greed!" a small shopkeeper would pray. "Help me to be kind!" "Help me to be serene!" The cries of millions of Japanese who believed in the power of the bells, who believed in the merciful power of Buddha.

The girl sat quietly, moved by the sound and by the deep tradition belonging to the night. She sat face to face with herself, with the past, with her future. Impressions of the past year passed like a dream through her mind—"Please be more careful, Sachiko! Certainly it's not necessary to waste food . . ." ". . . the bath wasn't hot enough—spend more time fixing it tonight . . ." "Can't you be a little quieter after you go to your room? I couldn't sleep last night!" Or, the memories continued, "Try to please her, Sachiko. . . ." "Try to get along with her. . . ." "Don't you think that if you did things her way. . . ." Sometimes the memories came in the foreign accent of the missionary woman: "God is your heavenly Father. . . . he loves you. Jesus told us to love our enemies. . . . When you give your life to God, he will give you strength to overcome your difficulties. . . ."

Over and over the memories whirled and danced through her head. "Do this!" "Can't you do this?" "If you do this . . . !" Suddenly her head ached and the conflicting questions grew almost too much to bear. The bells continued to toll. As she listened, she began to remember the hatred she had held. She had hidden it, tried to keep it under control, but it was there, nevertheless. It shook her. It tore her apart.

Even when she thought she had it conquered, it suddenly would not let her sleep. How many nights she had lain sleepless, thinking only of how some day she would not have to bear the strain and humiliation of being a servant in the home of her husband. The memory caused her hands to shake and her throat to tighten. It's eating me up, she thought suddenly, sitting very still. It's making me sick!

The calm of desperation settled over her. She felt as if a mask were covering her face, making it impossible to express the torment that burned in her body. "I feel as if I were dead," she said dully. "I feel as if the best part of me—everything good and happy—were dead." She forgot the future, for the future held nothing for her except work and submission to her husband's mother. The bells tolled on, but she found no deliverance, nothing to drive the hatred and fear from her heart, nothing to give her life again. For just a moment, her husband's face passed before her. She felt a sudden overwhelming rush of love. It kept her from complete despair. If it were gone, she would cease to live as a person and would become only a shell. She clung to her love, held on to it, until with a sigh she dropped her head in her arms and slept—slept until the bells stopped tolling and the front door rattled, signaling the return of her husband and mother-in-law from their midnight trip to the temple.

"Sachiko, go to the store and get some *okashi* and *osushi.*" Yoshiko Suzuki closed the door between the kitchen and the family room, but the high-pitched voices of the relatives from Kyushu could be heard clearly through the thin walls. "Hurry, won't you? It's embarrassing not to have anything in the house ready for them, but *shikata ga nai,* it can't be helped!" Her cheeks were faintly red with controlled excitement, and she looked about her distractedly. "Use the good tea cups and the lacquer tray. We don't want to appear poor relatives!"

Sachiko slipped on her wooden clogs in place of the slippers she wore in the kitchen and hurried down the street. It was warm. Already the cherry blossoms were beginning to bloom along the sides of the street. The branches of the trees formed an archway over her, and now and then a flower fell like snow, brushing her face softly before it joined the others on the paved street. A bed of daffodils bordered a neighbor's walkway, and tiny buds had appeared on the maple trees. March was gone with its blustering winds and dust; soft, fragrant April had come. Sachiko's heart sang with the birds, sang for no other reason than that spring had come at last.

Sachiko chose sweets in the color and shape of pale pastel flowers, each with sweet bean paste in its center. Since they had special guests, she ordered rice balls with raw fish instead of the usual ones wrapped in seaweed. Then she made her way quickly back to the house through streets covered with the delicate pink of the blossoms. As quietly as she could, she returned to the kitchen through the back door and continued preparing the tea, placing the *okashi* on individual plates, two to each dish. Engrossed in her work, she paid no attention to the conversation that went on in the next room until she heard her name mentioned. I'll have to wait until they talk about something else before I can go in, she thought, and set the tray on the worktable. Automatically, her hands found work to do, but it was impossible to shut her ears to the words that found their way from the guest room. They talked freely, unaware that she stood on the other side of the wall, reluctantly listening.

"I'm sure it must be difficult for you." The nasal voice of Ichiro's cousin echoed loudly. "If you lived in the country, you might have been able to return her to her family."

"But even in the country, you don't hear of that a great deal now," insisted Yoshiko Suzuki. "*Yappari,* a mother-in-law doesn't have any rights anymore."

"That's true. Young people certainly don't appreciate their elders now as they did in the old days. It's too bad." The old man cleared his throat self-consciously.

"Oh, Ichiro is a good son. He tries to listen to what I say. But she's got him completely fooled. She's turned my son from me!" Her voice was quiet, but it carried to the kitchen where the girl stood, all pretense of working gone, her cheeks flushed with shame. "She fools him with soft words. I'm almost embarrassed to live in the same house with them."

The clock ticked in the silence of the room for a full minute.

"You don't have to put up with that," the piercing high voice of the woman answered her. "There are things you can do to stop that."

"What?"

"Find work for her to do when he is at home."

"But Ichiro will be angry."

"He may for a while, but it will be the best thing for him. He'll appreciate it and remember it later. That boy won't forget what you did for him after his father died. He's a good boy."

"I get so tired sometimes," Sachiko heard her mother-in-law say bitterly. "I try to teach her to do things properly, but it's almost impossible. She has a strong will, that girl has. You wouldn't think so to look at her—so quiet and sullen—but she tries to get her way."

"It's too bad you didn't find out during the investigations. Didn't your go-between tell you anything of this?"

"I think the family tricked Kawaguchi San. Kawaguchi San is a good friend of mine. She would tell us if she had found anything undesirable. But it's difficult to discover faults of disposition through an investigation."

"Hmmmm."

"We checked her background. Her family is a good family and her father is well respected. We couldn't find anything in her school record which was against her. And everyone told us that she was a fine type of girl."

"It's too bad. Sometimes you don't really know people until you begin to live with them."

"But I have to live with her the rest of my life!"

A sympathetic silence followed. Trembling, Sachiko sat down in the doorway, the closed paper door the only thing separating her from the rest of the house. Her hands shook; she looked at them unseeingly, then thrust them under her apron.

"In the country you wouldn't have to put up with this sort of thing," the cousin repeated vehemently. She paused. Then, continuing carefully, she said, "I hope you won't think we are being rude, but *Ojiisan* and I are concerned about the family." A grunt of agreement came from the old man. The woman leaned forward. "Yoshiko San," she went on, her voice lowered almost to a whisper, "don't you think it is about time that Ichiro had a child—a boy to carry on the family name?"

"I . . ."

"Kenichiro was killed in the war, and the rest of the family were girls. We're afraid the name of Suzuki will die out completely. Ichiro is the only one on whom we can build any hope."

"They've been married for two and one-half years now," Yoshiko Suzuki spoke softly, but her voice carried bitterly to the kitchen. "I'm beginning to wonder if they can have children. Lazy, willful, a schemer—and now unable to fill the place in the family she is obligated to fill!" Her voice rose furiously. "What have I done that such evil should follow me and my family? It is almost more than a person can bear. Every day that I live in this house with her, I feel more as if I were an outsider in my own home!"

"See that she goes to a doctor right away. I would look into that, Yoshiko San!"

"I won't take her!"

"Of course not! Have her own mother take her."

They sat silent for a long time. "Sometimes I think that this house is cursed," Sachiko heard her husband's mother say finally. "We took care in building it. Ichiro laughed when I insisted that no windows should be placed facing the northeast. He said that is purely superstition." She paused. "My friend, Kawaguchi San, tells me that the addition to the kitchen is the cause of our misfortune. I don't know. Perhaps that is the problem. At any rate, something has gone wrong. But how could I know that?" she cried suddenly. "I trusted the carpenter. I have not studied such things. Is it my fault that evil has come from the Devil's Gate?"

"That is true. You have to be careful about things like that," the old man agreed slowly. "I once knew a family that had nothing but sickness and death—just because they were careless about building their house."

Sachiko sat on the doorsill, looking about the kitchen numbly. She saw the pans, the dishes, the unpainted walls, but all seemed like part of a bad dream. "I'll wake up and find that this never happened," she told herself. "Ichiro will come home and then I'll know that everything is the same. We'll close the door to our room and forget about the coldness in the rest of the house. We'll laugh and love and pay no attention to what the rest of the world thinks and says."

But inside herself, she knew that everything would never be the same again. Today would change things—would change them all. Until now the feelings had not been expressed in words. When said they became stronger. There would be no turning back from a decision voiced in the presence of representatives of the family—even distant relatives. Suddenly, she wished intensely that she were sure that Ichiro's feelings were strong enough to keep this day from making a change in their relationship. Her stomach tightened with pain, and fear swept over her as she stood up to light the fire under the teakettle.

The door opened and she turned, startled. Her mother-in-law stood there, and her face was flushed with anger. "Sachiko! We've waited a long time for tea. Please bring it in right away."

There was an unnatural, waiting silence in the guest room where the relatives sat. Aware that they listened, the older woman raised her voice with pretended severity, while her eyes glanced first at her daughter-in-law's guilty face, then swept to the teapot where the water did not yet boil. "What have you been doing? Did you stop to talk on the way at your friend's house?"

Frozen, unable to move, her eyes downcast and her heart thudding, Sachiko stood feeling unbearably afraid of the woman who stood above her. She waited, her tongue silent, until the door closed once again and then leaned against the wall and covered her face with her hands. The tears streamed over her fingers and wet the palms of her hands and her cheeks. Silently, she wept, her shoulders shaking. Her body was suddenly so weak that her legs could hardly hold her.

From the next room came an audible whisper. "Was she there?" A pause. "It's too bad she heard us, but she has to know sometime. Now you won't have to tell her."

The pots in the kitchen glared at her. The pale green of the sweets mocked her, and the teapot gurgled and laughed. "It's too bad . . . too bad. . . ."

In the guest room the relatives began to talk serenely about the weather and the cherry blossoms.

CHAPTER NINE

THEY CAME BACK from visiting the doctor earlier than they had expected. "Come in for a while, Sachiko," her mother said. "We haven't been able to talk at all since you've been married."

Sachiko hesitated. "I really need to get back."

"When does she expect you?"

"She didn't say, but if she knew that I stopped to talk, she would be furious." She looked with longing toward her parents' home, then said decisively, "I'll stay for a while."

When she entered the *genkan* she smelled again the odor of medicines that always permeated her father's office. He heard them come in and thrust his head around the edge of the office door, smiling at her with the special smile he always reserved for her.

"I'm almost through with this patient. Have your mother make you some tea."

She returned his smile, nodded in agreement, and went down the hall. She had always loved the large family room when she was a child, and now as she entered a feeling of familiarity and security swept over her. The afternoon sun filled it with warmth, while outside a bird sang in the stillness of the garden. She sat in the veranda in a bamboo chair, leaned her head back and closed her eyes. If only I could always feel this peace, this restfulness, I would never complain again, she thought. A bee buzzed just below the veranda, lit on a fully opened blossom of an azalea plant, then flew on to a bed of flowers. Wrapped in the warm cocoon of her parents' love and the memories of the house, she could almost pretend that she need never go back to the other again.

I would sleep and sleep and sleep, she thought drowsily. I would eat only what I want to eat and do what I want to do. But suddenly the clatter of teacups in the room made her open her eyes and she sat up, dazed, as if she had awakened from a beautiful dream only to learn that it was not real. "I"ll have to go back," she said to herself with dread. "I'll have to go back—there's no other way."

Her father came into the room and she turned her head to watch him. His face had grown older, but it held a wisdom she had not noticed before. He wiped his hands on a towel and sat on a cushion by the table. "Come, Sachiko! We want to hear how you have been getting along."

She stood, stretched slowly, then walked to the table, feeling the smooth warmth of the mats against her feet. The teacup she had used as a student stood in her place; her hands went around it naturally and an almost irresistible desire to stay here where she was loved took hold of her.

"I haven't done too much of anything," she said a trifle unsteadily, raising her eyes to his and then lowering them quickly before tears could fill them.

"Are things any better?"

"No."

"We're sorry. If we had known that things would be so difficult, we would never have consented to your marriage with him."

"It's not Ichiro—if we were living by ourselves, I don't think we would have any problems."

"Sachiko," her mother said, coming into the room from the kitchen, "doesn't Ichiro San realize what she is doing to you?" She set a tray of fruit on the table and poured another cup of tea.

Sachiko looked at her mother and thought, Has she forgotten the time she cried in the back of the house when Grandmother took me to the *Shichi-go-san* celebration at the shrine? Has she forgotten how hard she worked while we children were small? She sat silent for a moment, then said gently, "He knows, Mother, but he doesn't want to hurt her."

"Doesn't want to hurt her! Nothing could hurt that woman! He's afraid of her, that's what it is!"

"That may be so," Sachiko admitted patiently.

"Don't you get any time for yourself—any time to rest?"

"I used to, but since the relatives from Kyushu came to visit, I haven't been able to at all." She added slowly, "They thought she was too easy on me."

"That would never happen. She's a demon—that's what she is! A demon full of evil!"

"Now, that's a rather strong way to put it," her father interrupted firmly. "There are a lot of mothers-in-law who are not very understanding. Perhaps the reason we are upset by this is because Sachiko is our daughter." He turned to Sachiko, "Do you have money to use for yourself?"

She flushed, then answered softly, "There aren't too many things I need."

"But do you have a little to use?" he persisted.

"No, Ichiro gives his mother money every month for the house and food, and so I don't handle the money." She glanced up, saw the concern on their faces, then added quickly, "I don't think Ichiro keeps very much for himself, though. I think she keeps most of it; once or twice I've heard him asking her for money." She was still for a long time; her fingers caressed the design on the edge of her cup. She felt her eyes fill with tears. "But I heard something a day or so ago which hurt me more than anything else," she said finally. "Ichiro told me that his mother wanted me to leave him."

"Oh, Sachiko!"

"I couldn't believe that she would go so far. If I did leave, the whole neighborhood would know, and the family would never be able to face their friends again.

But she hates me so much that she would rather face humiliation than to have me in the house."

"That would be even worse for you." Her mother's voice was dull with pain.

"Yes, if I had to leave, I couldn't stand to live."

"Did she say you had to go?"

"According to what he told me, she wants me to leave, but he won't agree to it."

"And yet he would let her practically kill you with work!" Angrily, her mother swept the empty teacups onto the tray. "He cares enough for you to have you around when he wants you, but he doesn't care enough to protect you from her."

"I think the man is just weak."

Sachiko glanced quickly at her father, but his eyes were fixed on the garden. Did he remember her mother's cries in the night?

"He is young. Perhaps he will become a stronger person with a little more experience," her father finished.

Sachiko sat quietly, her hands clasped before her on the table. When she finally spoke, it was almost with reluctance—as if she did not care to speak of her husband or her mother-in-law but something drove her to continue. "He won't let me leave, but even so, staying there now is terribly hard. She complains that I spend too much for food when I go shopping—she says I buy too fine a grade of meat. Yet, when I buy a cheaper grade, she tells Ichiro that I am not fixing the meals so that they taste well enough. I try to be careful, but she notices if I eat very much and tells me I am being greedy."

As if he had not been listening to her at all, her father turned to Sachiko suddenly and said, "I want to give you some money so that you will have some to use for things you need. We don't want you to be completely without money."

"Father, really, there isn't any need for me to have money."

"We want you to have it. Wait a minute and I'll get it."

They watched him cross the room and open the door, and then heard his steps go down the hall toward his office. When he was gone, her mother turned to her. "If you can't have children, she will make your life miserable."

"Yes, I know." Suddenly, she clung desperately to her mother's arm, and sobbed, "Mother, I'm afraid of her! What shall I do?"

Her mother held her, stroked her hair gently. The sun moved on toward the west, the afternoon began to draw to a close, and the sound of the girl's weeping echoed through the room and out into the garden. The birds stopped their singing, and a cloud passed over the sun. Gradually her body grew still, but she lay with her head on her arms, her face wet and her heart sick.

"Sachiko, learn to bend. Don't stand against her—you will only break. Do your best to be kind. Perhaps you will help her to be kinder." Her mother spoke as though she had heard the words before, as if sometime, somewhere else, many years ago, her own mother had so spoken to her. "Be a lady. Don't let your feelings show even if things become unbearable.

"Remember the honor of our family and of the family into which you have been received. The Suzuki family is an honorable one and an old one. You must strive to be a good member of it, even if others in the family are not. It hasn't been easy for you these two years. The future won't be easy either, but remember that for generations the lot of the Japanese woman has been that of serving and of giving comfort. It may be that through you peace will come to Ichiro and his mother—one never knows. And even if it shouldn't come, you will only hurt yourself more by rebelling against the difficult circumstances in which you find yourself."

She lay silently—not speaking, but letting the words of her mother, the wisdom of the ages, find their way into her mind. A new strength came to her. She thought to herself, "I am not alone. Others have had the same trouble as mine, and some are still experiencing it. My mother went through her difficult times and became a strong person in spite of them. I must do the same."

Her mother's words echoed through her mind. "Bend, don't break. Give, and don't expect to receive. You will find happiness by becoming a part of the host of women who live unseen, whose strength is not known though it is there holding the family together. Without you the family could not live. They may not appreciate you, but remember, you are important. For you to give up would mean that the family would suffer." All the times her mother had talked to her about the duties of marriage flashed through her mind. If Mother has taught me nothing else, she thought, she has taught me this philosophy of surrender—a surrender that is not really surrender. A seeming compromise with the unconquerable, making it possible for one, by using patience and kindness and service, in reality to conquer.

She raised her head from her arms, her eyes still blinded with tears. She smiled, and her mother smiled in return. Suddenly, she felt closer to her mother than she had ever felt before. She wanted to tell her what she felt, but the words did not come easily. Instead, she said with a rush of feeling, "Mother, I do want a child. I want a child for Ichiro's sake—for his family's sake. But I want it for myself, too. I want to teach it to do all the things you taught me to do. I want to help it to be happy, to grow up to be good and strong, just as you taught me. I . . ."

She glanced up and saw her father in the doorway, the words she wanted to say driven from her by the look on his face. "Sachiko, don't count too much on having a child. You may be disappointed."

"Why?" The shared feeling was gone.

"I called Dr. Takeyama on the phone to find out the results of your examination. I know you have enough to think of without having this added to it, but the things he had to say didn't sound too good. I don't want you to count on having a child so much that you will be disappointed if it shouldn't be possible."

"Did he say that I couldn't have one? Did he say there was no hope at all?" She spoke quietly, almost as if she were talking about a sore throat or a headache.

"He couldn't say positively since some of the results are not yet in, but he did say that there is a possibility that you may not be able to bear a child. He will mail the results to you in the next day or so. I blame myself," he went on, grief showing in every line of his face. "I should have examined you myself long ago, but sometimes it is so easy to think that one's own family will not have the problems other people do."

"They would not have taken your word for it, anyway," she answered slowly and bitterly. "That is why they insisted that I go to another doctor."

"Will she turn you out, now, Sachiko?" her mother asked anxiously.

"I don't know. It depends on how strongly Ichiro opposes her. I think she will try to make me leave." She stood, smoothed her hair, then picked up her purse from the floor. "I have to go. It's getting late."

"Try to come back as soon as you can. Insist that she let you come home for the *Obon* festival this summer. She hasn't let you come home at all—not even during the New Year's holidays. It's not right!"

"I'll try, but I doubt she will let me come home—not after what has happened."

"Well, try if you can."

They walked to the entrance with her and stood watching from the gate. She turned and looked back after she had walked a long way down the street. Even after she could see them no longer, after she had entered the station and stood on the platform waiting for an electric train, she remembered the new wrinkles in her father's face and the weariness in her mother's eyes.

CHAPTER TEN

THE NEXT DAY Sachiko sat in her room sewing. The house was quiet except for the sound of rain drumming against the windows and on the roof. A light burned in a lamp on the desk, and music from the radio filled the small room. She sat alone. Her mother-in-law had not yet returned from a visit to a friend. For the moment, the stillness of the darkened house, the music, and being by herself was enough to make her happy.

She picked up a blouse belonging to her mother-in-law, examined the tear in the seam, then selected thread to match the material. The music filled her with an almost dreamlike intoxication. She turned the knob on the radio so that it swept powerfully and joyfully into the room and on through the empty house. She forgot the blouse in her hands. It slipped to the floor, the needle half through a stitch, the thread a bit of color in the light of the lamp. Her hands resting in her lap, she sat transported beyond the walls of the room. The world she entered was one of eternal music and warmth and love. Her own world of every day seemed far away. The clock on the bookcase ticked on relentlessly, but she was not aware of it. Nor was she aware of the opening of the front entrance door. She did not see the older woman slip stealthily into the *genkan* and quietly take off her *geta*.

"Sachiko!"

The bubble broke. It broke amidst crying trumpets, the thunder of drums, and the shrill clash of her mother-in-law's voice. It broke and she sat horror-stricken, her guilty hands lying in her lap, the blouse untended on the floor. Like a nightmare, like a bad dream, the older woman's face swelled before her, the blue vein in her neck standing dark above the flushed skin.

"What are you doing?" The music danced above the screams. "Is this what you do when I go out?" Higher and higher rose the cries of the violins, no longer beautiful and soothing. "Turn off that radio!" She walked stiffly in front of Sachiko and with a sharp twist, turned it off herself.

Her voice in the silence was more terrible than it had been above the music. "No wonder you don't accomplish anything! No wonder I have to do the work after I get home!" Shaking with anger, she went again to the doorway. Sachiko picked up the needle with stiff fingers, tried to force it into the material of the blouse.

"Listen to me!"

The girl froze, her eyes pools of terror.

"Leave the mending for this evening. You can do it after the other work is done. If you do the washing now, it will be ready to hang out early tomorrow morning." She started into the hallway, then turned to say, "And don't touch that radio again. You have other things to do—more important things than listening to that about which you know nothing."

Her fingers trembling, Sachiko folded the clothes and slipped them into a net bag. Then pushing the sleeves of her white housewife's apron up on her arms, she gathered clothing to wash.

It was cold in the outdoor washroom. The wind blew the rain under the roof, wetting her face and clothing. She worked quickly, rubbing, rinsing, wringing the clothes. The cold water made her hands numb. She placed the wet clothes in a wooden tub and carried them into the kitchen. Her mother-in-law glanced briefly at her, then down at the cutting board where she was preparing vegetables. Handing the knife to Sachiko, she said shortly, "Here, you finish this. I'm going to work in the other room for a while."

Sachiko set the tub in the corner and went to the cutting board. The vibrant green of the spinach leaves blended with the orange and white of the carrots and radishes. Without realizing she was talking aloud, before she could stop herself, Sachiko exclaimed, "Ichiro doesn't like carrots. He told me so the other day. He said never to cook carrots again!"

"Cook what I tell you to! I guess I should know what Ichiro likes or doesn't like!"

Guiltily, Sachiko turned back to her work. She resolved never to say what she thought again.

It was still raining when Ichiro came into the entrance. Sachiko greeted him at the door and took his coat and briefcase. He went by her without speaking. He was irritated with everything—the rain that would not stop, the cold, and most of all with a fellow teacher who had opposed him that day. Although he would never have admitted it, he was also unhappy about coming home to this house where his mother babied him and his wife went about with fear constantly in her eyes.

He changed from his wet clothes into a padded kimono, complaining as he did so. Sachiko listened in sympathetic silence as she helped him with his clothes and hung them to dry. When he had changed, she left him sitting near a brazier with a newspaper, not far from where his mother sat.

He was feeling almost happy again until he saw Sachiko bring in the carrots. "I thought I told you not to fix carrots anymore. I don't like them, and I don't want them on our table!"

Sachiko glanced uneasily at her mother-in-law. Not a muscle moved in the older woman's face. She sat silently regarding the steam that rose from the dish, chewing thoughtfully and deliberately.

"Sachiko, didn't you hear what I said?" Ichiro's face

flushed with irritation. "Take them back into the kitchen."

She glanced once more at his mother and then slipped quietly into the kitchen, the dish of carrots carried before her on the tray. Why didn't she tell him she wanted the carrots prepared? she thought. She let him think that it was I who planned the meal. She set the carrots on the cutting board and went back into the eating room.

"It is too bad to waste food. We should have thought of you before cooking carrots," her mother-in-law was saying. "I remember how as a boy you would hardly eat them."

"Well, she should have known better! I told her the other day not to fix them anymore!" The food was too sweet, and the trouble over the carrots made him remember his difficulties with the teacher. Suddenly, intensely irritated, he called for tea, drank it quickly and left the table long before his mother and wife were finished. He left them staring uncomfortably at their plates, aware of his presence in the next room, noticing every sound he made—the click of the light switch, a book laid down on the desk, the creak of the chair when he sat down to study.

Sachiko cleared the table and washed the dishes. Then, seeing that her mother-in-law was not in the eating room, she slipped through it and into the next room.

"Ichiro," she whispered tentatively and knelt beside his desk. His forehead wrinkled in concentration, but he gave no other indication that he knew of her presence. "Ichiro . . ." the light shone on her face, brought the soft lines of her cheek into clear relief against the semidarkness of the room. His anger left him. He felt only very tired and unhappy.

"Why don't you try to do as I ask you to do, Sachiko? You know I asked you not to make carrots. I told you not to make the food so sweet. You make me think that you don't want to please me at all!"

How could she tell him that she had to cook as his mother told her to cook? How could she tell him that if she had her own way, she would do everything in her power to please him? Knowing that she sounded as if she were only offering excuses, she said slowly, "Your mother likes things sweet . . ."

"And it is more important to please my mother than to please me?"

"I want to please you."

"Then, try a little harder." His mood changed, became lighter. "Let's forget about it. Let's let this night at home be a happy one." He turned in his chair, put his arm around her and drew her up beside him. "It is early yet. We have lots of time to talk, and you can help me with some of these papers. I have missed your help."

"You aren't angry with me, then?"

"Angry?"

"Oh, Ichiro, you know how things have been lately!"

"You mean about Mother's wanting you to leave? You know I would never let you go."

"I don't want to leave you." Her eyes met his and the warmth that flowed from them almost blinded him. He touched her face with his forefinger. It moved along the curved line of her cheek to the back of her neck and rested there, the palm of his hand flat against her back.

"Don't ever leave me," he said. "Even if we cannot have children, we can still be happy together. It is you and I who are important—just the two of us. No one else matters." But she knew that even though he spoke with unconcern regarding the child they might never have, he desired above all else to have a son to carry on the family name. Because he thought of her and not of himself, because he did not blame her, she loved him more than she ever had before.

"Sachiko!" querulously, the voice of her mother-in-law came to them from the other room. "Sachiko, please come here."

He caught her as she turned to go. "Don't leave me tonight!"

"I have to, Ichiro." Her eyes pleaded with him to understand.

"Don't go tonight. I need you."

"But, Ichiro, your mother is calling. If I don't go, she will be angry."

"You won't be back until late. It will be just as it has been every other night."

"I'll try. Really, I will!"

"Sachiko, if you go tonight, you'll be sorry!"

Hopelessly, she tried to reason with him. "Don't you understand what kind of web I'm caught in? I have to do what your mother wants me to do, but yet you expect me to please you, too. You and your mother are fighting against each other, and I'm the one in the middle. Oh, Ichiro, please help me! I'm trying to do the best I can."

Suddenly angry, he thrust her from him. She stumbled and fell against the edge of the desk. "I'm tired of being a go-between in the fights and disagreements between my mother and my wife. I don't even look forward to coming home anymore. This isn't a home. It is nothing but a place where we argue and pull each other apart!" He turned back to the desk. "I mean it! If you go in and spend the evening with her, you'll be sorry!" He picked up his pen and began scanning the papers on the desk.

She longed to run to him—to forget the persistingly nagging voice in the other room. But she knew that if she did, she would be making it impossible to remain here in this house. She knew that if she chose her husband and rejected her mother-in-law, sooner or later her mother-in-law would force her to leave. Her eyes were dry, but her chest felt heavy with unshed tears. She took one more look at him, memorized every part of his rangy, attractive form—his strong, stubborn face

—and carried it with her into the next room where her husband's mother waited.

Throughout the next two hours while she massaged and thumped her mother-in-law's body, and even after the older woman was asleep, she asked herself over and over, "Could I have done anything else? Did I do something to make him think that I did not care for him? Is it my fault that I cannot get along with either of them?" Until late into the night she sat in the eating room under a dim light, finishing the mending she had started that afternoon and thinking of the events of the evening. When she was finally able to lay the sewing aside, each piece repaired neatly, her husband's in one pile and her mother-in-law's in another, she knew that it was too late to undo the evil that had made its way into the house that day. Her mother-in-law slept at last. The house was hers and hers alone, but it was too late. For her husband was also asleep.

The women were not worried when Ichiro failed to come home at his usual time the following evening. "Ichiro's late," Sachiko said absently to herself and then thought only of finding some way to keep the rice warm. But when dinnertime passed and still he did not return, she became uneasy. Several times she went to the front entrance, opened the door, and looked out into the darkening walkway toward the street. Shiro thumped his tail against the side of his house, but there was no sign of his master's coming. Sachiko pushed the door shut and stepped outside quietly. The warm odor of early summer permeated the air. Scents of crushed roses, of young leaves, and a musty hint of the beginning rainy season filled the garden.

Footsteps approached along the lane from the street. They slowed gradually until she thought they would turn in at the gate, but then they continued steadily on past the gate and stopped at the neighbor's house instead. She paused a moment longer, then reluctantly went back into the brightness of the eating room.

Her mother-in-law looked up from her work. "He's not coming yet?" It was more of a statement than a question. She examined Sachiko's face, then returned to her work, her lips pursed and a frown on her forehead.

Sachiko picked up a ball of thread and her crochet needle and looked at them thoughtfully. "Was it because of last night that he is late getting home?" she asked herself. "He was angry with me, and I'm sure he hasn't forgotten it." Her stomach ached. I'm hungry, she thought. In the kitchen the rice still steamed in the *okama* and the vegetables were waiting on individual dishes to be carried to the eating room, but they dared not eat until the master of the house returned.

"He has found more interesting places to be," her mother-in-law's voice broke shockingly into the midst of her thoughts. "He's gotten tired of you, and now he's found other ways to enjoy himself."

Sachiko felt her lips tighten, but she made no answer to the other woman's taunts.

Putting down her work, Yoshiko Suzuki turned so that she could look directly into Sachiko's face. "You've turned him away from his home," she continued harshly. "You—with your soft ways. He wasn't satisfied with you long, was he?" A cricket chirped in the kitchen. Sachiko bent her head lower, so that her face was almost covered by the crochet work and the needles. "Do you know what he is probably doing now?" The woman's face grew bitterly hard and her voice was full of hate. "He's found some friend and they have gone to Tokyo. Right now he is sitting in an eating room with a couple of young geisha. They are laughing and talking; he is telling them things he has never told you!" She stirred restlessly. "Did you think you could succeed in turning him away from me? Did you think that you could make him forget his mother and the things I did for him? If you did, you're wrong, now, and you know you are wrong! Do you think he wants you now—you who cannot even give him a child?" She saw Sachiko start with surprise and added quickly, "Oh, yes, I saw the letter that came from the doctor today. I was expecting it, and it was just as I thought. You don't have any rights in this family, now. You lost all your rights when you failed to give Ichiro a child!" She stood up abruptly and left the room.

Sachiko sat frozen, unable to move. The letter was in my purse, she thought. I remember putting it in my purse before I started dinner this evening. Suddenly, she realized that nothing was sacred to herself alone. Every move she made was under observation and appraisal. Every remark was weighed and twisted to be used against her. She felt stripped naked of all personal feelings and thoughts until nothing was left of her but a dry shell.

"Love your enemies and pray for those who persecute you."[1] The teachings of Jesus in her Bible, which lay hidden in the back of her closet, pushed their way through her confused mind. "You have heard that it was said, 'An eye for an eye and a tooth for a tooth.' But I say to you, Do not resist one who is evil. But if any one strikes you on the right cheek, turn to him the other also; and if any one would sue you and take your coat, let him have your cloak as well."[2] Love her? Forgive her? "But I can't," she cried desperately. "I can't do it!"

Almost as if she were sleepwalking, as if she were dreaming, she went to her room, drew out the money her father had given her from underneath a pile of books in the back of the closet. Then, hardly aware of what she was doing, she slipped out of the house and down the path to the street.

She had been gone only a short while when her husband returned home, his hair disheveled and his eyes dull from drinking. He did not know, and his mother

[1]Matthew 5:44
[2]Matthew 5:38–40

did not tell him, that his wife was gone. Calmly, the old woman began her preparations for bed. It is better this way, she thought. It is better that we pretend that she never was here at all. But she forgot that her son in the next room might not find it so easy to forget. The quiet of the night settled about the house, but it was not quite the same as it had been before the girl came there to live.

CHAPTER ELEVEN

HER HAIR WAS IN HER EYES and she cried as she ran. Here and there a street light made a small oasis of brightness in the night, but between them the shadows lurked in the doorways and behind the hedges. A drunk walked the middle of the street, and she knelt behind a fence until the sound of his uneven footsteps could no longer be heard. A familiar gate loomed before her. She shoved the door aside and stepped into a garden; then, panting heavily, she went to the entrance of the house.

"Matsuoka San!" She waited, listening. "Matsuoka San!" Footsteps sounded from within the house. A door opened.

"Who is it?"

"Suzuki Sachiko. Let me in, would you?"

The latch was loosened and she slipped inside, closing the door behind her.

"Sachiko San, what are you doing here?" Her friend's eyes were startled and puffy with sleep. In the dim light which came through a window in the back of the house, Sachiko could see sleeping mattresses covering the floor of the room. From far back in the room came the sound of snoring; then someone stirred and talked softly in his sleep.

"I've run away. I just couldn't take it any longer!"

"Honto ni?"

Sachiko nodded.

"What will you do? If you stay here, they will know where you are and come after you, won't they?"

"I don't know. I didn't know any other place to go."

"I could find a place for you, but I'm afraid they would find you here." She paused, then continued curiously, "Are you leaving him? Aren't you ever going back?"

"I don't know," Sachiko began to cry again. "I don't know what I'm going to do. I should kill myself!"

"Oh, no! That won't help matters any. We'll figure something out." She was silent again. "I know," she said at last, "the missionary! Roberts Sensei! Wait just a minute! I'll change my clothes."

A breeze blew through the crack in the door. Sachiko shivered, as much from exhaustion as from the coolness of the night.

It was late. The busses had stopped running. The girls half ran, half walked the distance to the western part of town. Their footsteps rang on the deserted streets. Several times they had to step aside when a speeding taxi passed them. Usually bustling and noisy during the day, the streets were now silent. *Amado* were drawn across the windows and verandas of the stained wooden houses, giving them a peculiarly shut-eyed look. The litter of bicycles, small children in *geta*, and vegetable carts was gone, making the roadway seem wide. They crossed over a bridge, and the world shook for a moment as a train passed beneath them. Its lights grew gradually dim, their eyes following it down the track and on across the river to the country beyond. A dog barked at them, a cat ran across the road; other than that the world seemed to be completely unaware of their passing.

The moon seemed to shine unusually bright, especially when they drew near to the community where the church was. Above the sleeping houses, the steeple rose and on the very top of it shone the white cross. They made their way across the kindergarten playground toward the missionary's house.

"The house is dark, Matsuoka San. I hate to disturb them."

"It is all right. They'll understand," Matsuoka said, pressing her finger on the doorbell.

A light flashed on, illuminating them in a bright patch of light.

"Matsuoka San and Suzuki San!" the missionary exclaimed as she opened the door. "Is something wrong?" She glanced quickly at Sachiko's tear-streaked face and then said gently, "Come in and we'll talk about it."

They seated themselves on cushions in the Japanese-style room. Slowly, hesitantly, Sachiko began to tell the missionary the things which had taken place in her husband's house. Roberts Sensei listened, only occasionally asking a question. When Sachiko had finished, the missionary sat silently for a moment, her eyes thoughtful.

"Do you wish to go back to him?" she said finally, asking the same question Matsuoka had asked.

"I don't know," Sachiko shook her head in bewilderment. "If I didn't have to live with his mother, I wouldn't be unhappy at all. But as long as she lives, it will be unbearable for me to live there."

The missionary paused again and then said, her eyes looking directly into Sachiko's, her voice deliberate and slow. "I want to ask you a question, but I do not want you to answer it now. Think about it for a while." The light-blue eyes held a peculiar fascination for Sachiko. They caught her up in a continuous circle of warmth and intimacy—of expectation and challenge. She waited, breathing a little lighter, a little quicker than was usual.

"Are you sure that all of your problem is your mother-in-law's fault? Are you sure that you would be completely happy if you did not live with her?"

"I—"

"No. Don't answer now. Think about it, and tomorrow we will talk together about it. It is not easy to talk when you are tired and upset. After you have had a good night's sleep, we will have plenty of time to talk.

You are sure you don't want to go home tonight?"

"Yes, I'm sure."

"Then, we will be glad to have you stay here with us. I'll make a bed for you here in this room."

"Thank you so much," Sachiko said softly.

Long after Matsuoka had left and the *futon* were laid out—long after the lights were out and the missionary had gone back to her own room to sleep—Sachiko lay awake and tried to sort out the confused thoughts that ran through her mind. She remembered the first time she had ever come to this house for the Bible study-cooking class. Everything had been so strange. She had watched and listened but had understood little of what the *sensei* had said. But because she had wanted to know more about the missionary woman and because she enjoyed being with the other women, she continued to come.

It was her only opportunity to get away from the house where she was finding it more and more difficult to have thoughts and feelings which belonged to herself alone. It was her only chance to escape into a world where people laughed unashamedly, where they were not afraid to speak of their own problems or happy experiences in the presence of others. She did not understand, but there was an atmosphere in the class that held her. It held her and would not let her go. When she returned to her home after the meetings, she always felt happier. Still she did not think she was interested in learning of the American religion. She sat through the teachings of the Bible only because it was a part of the class and not because she particularly wanted to learn.

But as she had begun to listen, she had also begun to wonder and to question things she had taken for granted. She remembered the casual worship of her family before the *butsudan* and the Shinto god-shelf which had its place of honor high on the wall in her home, but which was forgotten except at festivals or when some difficulty forced the family to seek help. Many times she had dressed in her best clothes and had gone with her parents and her grandmother to visit the shrine on a festival day. "But it was more for fun than for worship that I went," she said to herself.

The gaily decorated stalls selling trinkets, charms, and special foods seemed to have little connection with worship. True, her parents had gone to the shrine to worship, but once they had cleansed their mouths with the water in the *mitarashi*, rung a bell to gain the attention of the gods, prayed for good health, good luck, or a prosperous life, they turned from the shrine and forgot the worship in the excitement of eating and mingling with the crowds. They listened to a fortuneteller explain a chart which was covered with pictures of disasters to be avoided by following his teachings. A goldfish dealer caught tiny orange-and-black fish in a net and put them in plastic bags so Sachiko could carry them home. At last, tired but happy, and carrying a branch with good luck charms tied to it—a fish, old Japanese money to bring prosperity, black and white dice—she followed her parents to their home. But the day had little religious meaning for her. It was only a time of eating delicious food, going to an exciting place, and wearing her best clothes.

She remembered the large *daruma* which had sat high on a shelf in her parents' home. Its eyes were always darkened, for there was usually joy in that home. A *daruma* sat on a shelf in her mother-in-law's home, too. Legless, his round fat body was joined to his head by a thick neck. But his white-ringed eyes were not yet darkened. They were untouched by any paint, just as they had been when her mother-in-law had brought the figure from the temple during the *Setsubun* Festival that previous year. Her mother-in-law said that she had no joys yet which would make it possible for her to paint the eyes of the *daruma*. Sachiko knew what she meant —no son had been born into the home since their marriage. The *daruma* was a daily reminder of her failure.

When she first heard the missionary speak of God, she had thought that Jesus—*Iesusama*—was another god to be added to the long list of gods worshiped by her people. But soon she began to realize that the missionary was not speaking of gods, but of one God. Christians believe that there is only one God. He is a Father who loves and cares for each one of his earthly children. But what of the other gods? she thought. What of Jizo Sama, of Buddha, of Ebisu Sama, of the many other gods of Buddhism and Shintoism? Was what she had been taught all her life false? Or were the Christians wrong in their beliefs? Yet, how could something which taught so much good be false?

She had begun to read her Bible. She had read of Jesus who healed the lepers, who taught that she must love and live for others. She read that this Jesus forgave those who did wrong to him. As the months went by, she began to feel that he had become almost real to her. She tried to do kind things, but when she failed she became discouraged.

"Christianity is a good teaching, but it is impossible to live like a Christian," she told herself after one particularly difficult day. "It is good to read the Bible. Certainly, it will help us to do better, but we cannot live as Christ did. It is impossible." So she struggled to be kinder, tried not to hate, but found herself hating as much as she had ever hated. She wanted to follow the good teachings of Jesus. She soon knew that she could not do so.

Sachiko lay on the *futon* in the missionary's house and thought of what the missionary had said. One God. A God who loves. A God who sent his Son into the world to teach, to live among the evils of the same world she lived in, to help people to know a way of life which was unselfish, clean, and full of love.

"Can it be true?" she asked herself. "Can it be true that such a God would care about me?" Her ears were closed to the sounds of the night outside. The noise of the American planes from the base nearby did not disturb her. She closed her eyes and as she did, she shut out the room from her mind. If I should serve a God like that, could some of the kindness and love of that God enter into me? Could I love my mother-in-law even though she hates me? And my husband—Ichiro, who did not come home. He had not come home, and all alone she had borne in her heart the terrible news which the letter had brought that day. When she had needed him most, he had not been there to encourage and love her. If he rejects me because I cannot give him a child, shall I still love him? She lay quietly; her eyes were dry, but the tears in her throat were achingly real.

"Are you sure that all your problem is your mother-in-law's fault?" The words of the missionary echoed in her mind over and over again. "If you did not live with her, would you be completely happy?"

Happiness! What was happiness, anyway? Had she been happy when, as a child, she had been cared for, loved, and taught to believe that the world was hers to have if she reached for it? But the world her father had given her—the world for which she had reached—had exploded into a thousand pieces. A broken balloon, but broken through no fault of her own. Broken and irreparable. Was this happiness?

Had she been happy, really happy, through her years at the university? She had studied hard, but a sense of loneliness, an indescribably bitter feeling of dissatisfaction had begun then in spite of her desire to learn and to cultivate as many skills as possible. She had prepared herself to become a wife, but had failed as one. She had tried for years to learn whatever would help her to become a good mother, but the gods had given her no child. A childless woman!

In the eyes of her family and friends, she had no purpose except that of serving. Service to her mother-in-law during her lifetime and to her husband and his family during the rest of her own life. She had no real right to personal interests. She had no right to make decisions of her own. She must obey and respect. She must make her own feelings subordinate to those with whom she lived.

She defended herself—argued with herself. "How could I have been to blame?" she cried inside, her lips soundlessly forming the words. "How could I have been at fault? No one told me what she was really like before I married. Haven't I tried to be kind to her even when she didn't return kindness? Haven't I tried to do things her way? I did the best I could," she tried to say to herself, but she knew that it had not been her best. For the hate had been there inside of her. It had been there while she had carried a smile on her lips. The hate had been there all the times she had meekly bowed and agreed outwardly with her husband's mother's words and opinions. She had hated until all traces of peace and happiness had been destroyed within her. And now she knew that either she must find a way to get rid of the hatred, or she would not be able to live with herself.

"Oh, God—God of the Christians—please help me." She prayed awkwardly, not knowing the proper way to form the words. She prayed as a small child does, slowly and carefully. "I can't live like this any more. If You really exist, help me to know You." The desperate need overwhelmed her so that she lay emotionally exhausted, hardly aware of her body nor of the tears that seemed to well up from her throat. "God, if you can give me peace and happiness, teach me how to serve You. Teach me to believe in You."

Suddenly her body relaxed. Her hand swept the tears away, and a smile passed over her face. She slept. It was the peaceful, childlike sleep of one who has found satisfaction. The tension and fear had disappeared. Trust had come in their place.

Emile Roberts yawned sleepily when she heard Bobby call, then rolled over and pulled the sheet up over her head.

"Mommie." She heard the pad of his bare feet on the hall floor. "Mommie, it's time to get up!"

She peered over the edge of the sheet with one eye. "Honey, it's not even six o'clock. Go back to bed for a little while!" He stood looking at her in dismay, the buttons on his pajamas coming loose, his face serious and disapproving. She laughed. "Oh, all right! Come in bed with Mommie for a little while."

Bobby grinned, threw his wiry little body on the bed and squirmed in between the sheets. She held him tight against her, felt his heart beating. He lay quiet for a moment, then wiggled a few inches from her. "There are some shoes in the *genkan!*"

"Yes."

"Whose are they?"

Whose are they? she echoed in her mind. "They belong to a lady who came to talk to Mommie," she answered gently. Whose shoes are they? she asked herself again. A young woman who came in the night for help, her face tight with tension. A young woman who is running away from her problems but who has nowhere to run. "Oh, dear God," Emile prayed silently, "how can I help her when I have never had to face persecution such as she has? How can I tell her what to do when I would not know what to do were I in her place?" Suddenly she stopped short, her mind clear and alert, her face and eyes still. But I can't tell her what to do, she thought in surprise. Telling her what to do will not solve her problems. Somehow, I will have to help her to make her own decision.

She looked down at her son, saw his eyes close and his face relax as he went to sleep in the circle of her arm. Beside her, her husband stretched, opened one eye cautiously, then went back to sleep.

From far down the road came the morning call of the *natto* seller. Nasal, almost haunting, her call echoed through the small houses in the community where *amado* were being opened, and a new day was begun. A bean curd seller came by on a bicycle, blowing his whistle.

"I've got to get up," she said to herself reluctantly, but having said it, she felt little inclination to do so. Carefully removing her arm from beneath Bobby's neck, she slipped out of the bed, put on a robe, and walked to the study at the far end of the house.

"God, help me to lead Suzuki San to find You. Teach her what Your will is for her life and then guide her and give her strength to face the consequences." She drew the drapes aside and stood looking out into the garden. "The responsibility is so great. I cannot do it by myself. Be present within our home this morning." The morning mists lifted, and the sun broke out in a blaze of glory above the tops of the stained wooden buildings. It reflected against the pine paneling of the room, and for a moment Emile Roberts' hair glowed red against the background of the curtains.

By the time breakfast was finished and the Roberts family and their guest had sung hymns together and prayed, they could hear the voices of the kindergarten children outside. Sachiko walked to the window and watched them playing on the swings and in the sand pile. She watched, and yet her mind was not upon what they were doing. Instead, she was thinking of the incidents which had taken place the previous night.

"Suzuki San, what will happen if you do not go home again?" Emile put down the plate she held in her hands, left the dishes on the table still unwashed, and came to stand beside the younger woman.

Sachiko bowed her head, avoiding the eyes of the missionary. "I don't know."

"Could you go home to your own parents?"

"No."

"You mean they wouldn't take you in?"

"They would take me in, but it would be difficult for them. I would only be a reminder of how my family had lost face. I wouldn't want to cause them more sorrow than I already have."

Emile drew her down to the window seat. "Have you thought about the questions I asked you last night?"

"Yes, I have thought about them," Sachiko said slowly.

"What did you think?"

Suddenly unable to translate her feelings into words, she sat silent, her eyes still downcast.

"If you had not had to live with your mother-in-law, could you have been happy—really happy, I mean?"

Sachiko shook her head.

"Why?" The missionary's eyes were warm and gentle. "Do you mean that something else is needed in your life before you can be happy?"

"I know that I cannot live as I have. I need some other help before I can live the kind of life I want to live."

The missionary smiled through her tears. "You do believe in the one, true God, don't you, Suzuki San?"

"Yes, I do." Sachiko paused. "For so long I came to the Bible class and did not understand. I tried to be kinder and to show more love to my mother-in-law, but the harder I tried, the more it seemed as if I had failed. I hated her, and I didn't have strength enough to get rid of my hatred. Then I wanted to kill myself, but my friend Matsuoka San helped me, and so I didn't do that. I think that if no one had helped me, I would have killed myself." A smile came into her eyes. "But last night, as I lay thinking about my problem and the questions you asked me to think about, I prayed to God and asked him to help me to believe. I know my prayer is answered."

"The Christian way is not easy."

"I know it isn't easy, but I am not happy without Christ. I tried to follow his teachings without accepting him into my life, and I failed. Because of that, I know that the Christian life is the only one in which I can find happiness."

The smile in Emile Roberts' eyes spread over her face. "I've prayed for you for a long time—ever since you started coming to the Bible class two years ago. I knew that you were not happy, but I didn't know what your trouble was. I am so happy that you have given your life to God."

"But I know so little. Please teach me, *Sensei.*"

"We will learn together." She paused thoughtfully. "Suzuki San, going back to your husband's home would not be easy, would it?"

Sachiko glanced out the window. "No, I would lose face by going back. It would be twice as hard to go back as to stay away, now." A stillness crossed her face, drove away the smile, leaving it bleak and tired.

"But doing the easy way will not always bring happiness," the missionary said softly.

"No, I have found that to be true." Sachiko thought of the times she had endured the pettiness of her mother-in-law's criticisms. It would not be easy to go back again. Her mother-in-law would laugh at her. Her husband would despise her. The neighbors would turn their heads and smile behind their hands, while gossip would travel the community as quickly as the wind blew. She would go shopping, and her friends would greet her, would smile at her, nothing but friendliness on their faces, but after she had passed by, they would turn to each other and begin talking about her and about the problem she had with her mother-in-law. Her trouble by now must certainly have become community news. But if I don't go back, she thought to herself, I will be running away. I would always feel that I had let this trouble overcome me. She straightened decisively and said calmly, "*Sensei,* I have to go back."

Outside the children no longer played in the swings. The playground was quiet. A white cat crossed in front of the empty swings, stopped cautiously to listen to the music of the piano that came from the classrooms in the church, then stepped daintily into the road.

"I thought you would go back." Emile Roberts smiled. "But I knew that it would be best that you thought so, too. It needs to be your own decision." She picked up a black leather Bible which lay beside her on the window seat. "Let's read the Bible and then talk with God about this decision you have made."

The words that she read remained in Sachiko's mind. God spoke to her and she answered with her life. Henceforth, she would not be alone. She would feel always the presence of her heavenly Father in a new and wonderful way.

CHAPTER TWELVE

As soon as Sachiko saw the ambulance before the lane that led to her own group of houses, she thought of her husband. A white ambulance flashing red lights stood with an open, waiting door. A group of children pressed against the windows, their wide eyes fixed on the empty bed inside the vehicle.

"Is someone hurt?" she asked the oldest child, then followed the direction her slim arm had pointed. Up a familiar path between the hedges, past a neighbor's house, and on to the gate which stood in front of her own house. It was a gate crowded now with people—the curious, the concerned, the vicariously sympathetic who in spite of their sympathy, felt sure that such things could never happen to them or to their families.

"Who is hurt?" she cried suddenly to a man standing by her. "Who's hurt?"

He stared curiously at her for a moment, then without answering, moved away to join the crowd.

I'll never be able to forgive myself, she thought almost hysterically as she made her way toward the house. I should never have run away last night. If it is Ichiro who is sick or hurt . . .

She stopped, looked down at the hand on her arm, then up at a familiar face. "Oh, Matsuoka San!" she cried desperately. "What has happened? No one will tell me. Is it Ichiro?"

"No, it's his mother." The hand tightened and drew her forward through the crowd. "Come. I'll help you to find him."

He was standing just inside the entrance. I should not have left him last night, she thought guiltily, seeing the pallor of his face. No matter what happened, I should not have done it!

She touched his arm gently. "Ichiro!"

"Oh, you're back." He seemed relieved. Then she was forgotten again as he stood waiting, his eyes fixed on the door which led to his mother's room.

"What happened?"

He turned toward her reluctantly. "Mother had a heart attack. I found her unconscious this morning beside her bed."

"But . . ."

"I'll tell you later." He moved aside and Sachiko caught a glimpse of a still white face, a body molded by the stretcher coverings. When she turned again, he was almost out of the *genkan*. "I'm going along. Try to get someone to take care of the house. Bring *futon* and things you will need to the hospital." Before she could nod he was gone, swallowed up by the crowd of neighbors who stood before the gate. Then the morning was filled with the scream of the ambulance siren, but after it had died away and she turned to face the judgment in the eyes of the waiting women, she almost wished that she had not had to stay.

"Where was the man's wife?" she heard one voice say. The woman's remark was made behind her hand, but it was loud enough for most of those standing near her to hear. "I didn't see her until just now. Doesn't she stay home and take care of the old woman? What a shame!" Sachiko turned quickly and entered the house, closing the entrance door after her.

The eating room was cluttered. She stood looking at it for a moment, then stooping, automatically straightened a cushion and picked up a newspaper that had fallen from the table. I've got to get the house cleaned and collect the things to be taken to the hospital, she thought almost wildly. And a *rusuban!* How will I ever find someone to stay in the house while we are gone?

A knock on the back door shattered the abnormal

stillness of the house. *"Chotto matte kudasai,"* she called and carried a tray of dishes with her to the kitchen.

"Sachiko San, it's Matsuoka."

Sachiko unlatched the door, and her friend almost fell into the room. "I came to the back door because I didn't want to go through that gang of gossiping women in the front!" She looked around at the uncleaned kitchen. "Is there something I can do?"

"Do!" Sachiko began to laugh, but her voice broke into a sob. "There's so much to do that I don't know where to start!"

Matsuoka looked at her, her eyes startled and concerned. Then, leading her unresistingly into the eating room, she said, "You have no business trying to clean the house when you feel like that. Lie down and rest while I clean the kitchen. Then we can gather the things together that you need to take to the hospital." She eased her gently onto the *tatami* floor and leaving the kitchen door open, began to wash the dishes in the sink outside.

The girl inside the house lay completely still. The *amado,* not yet drawn to let in the morning sun, caused dark shadows to drift across the *tatami*. Sachiko closed her eyes, but now and then she felt a muscle twitch nervously around her mouth. Her hands fingered the roughness of the matted floor. Outside, the dog whimpered once or twice, then was still.

If I had not run away from home, she thought with despair, would Ichiro's mother be ill—perhaps dying? Did she have the attack because I left? The questions pounded against the walls of her mind like the pendulum of a clock. If I hadn't done this—would this have happened? But there were no answers. Her head ached. Putting her hand to her eyes, she sought to close out the remembrance of the white face and the still form on the stretcher—the memory that haunted her. But I am responsible, she thought with horror. I am as responsible as if I had killed her!

Then, suddenly, into the quietness of the room, gently shoving aside all the silt of questions and tangles of guilt, came the soft words of the Scripture which the missionary had read that morning. "God is our refuge and strength, a very present help in trouble. . . . Be still and know that I am God."[1] . . . "But my God shall supply all your need according to his riches in glory by Christ Jesus."[2] The tension left her face and her body relaxed.

" 'I can do all things through Christ which strengtheneth me,' "[3] she repeated to herself softly. "Oh, God! Forgive me, for I have hated!" The words tore their way through her body, a searing flame of agony and self-examination. "I am guilty of hatred—of evil. Give me love—the hands of love so that I may care for the one I have hated."

There is love in the heart of God, she thought suddenly. There is love, and there is mercy. There is forgiveness. The missionary told me this, and I know that what she said is true. To love those who hate you, to do good to those who do evil—this I can do, not by my own power, but by the forgiving power and love of God. The feeling of quiet strength that came over her was a benediction—an answer to her prayer. She sat up, a smile on her face.

"You don't have to get up yet," Matsuoka said when she saw her standing in the doorway. "You'll need your strength later."

Sachiko paused, then answered softly, " 'I can do all things through Christ which strengtheneth me.' "

"What did you say?" Startled, her friend lay down the dish and wiped her hands, her eyes still fixed on Sachiko's face.

"I said I have all the strength I need."

"Sachiko San, have you lost your mind?"

---

[1]Psalm. 46:1, 10a [2]Philippians 4:19
[3]Philippians 4:13

The girl laughed. "No, Matsuoka San! I've regained my mind! I feel as if I were a completely different person." Seeing that her friend was becoming more and more concerned, she said quickly, "Have you ever heard Roberts Sensei talk of the peace of knowing you are forgiven?"

"Have you become a Christian?"

"Wait, let me explain what I mean." Sachiko picked up the dish and began washing it, her eyes fixed on the sink as she worked, her words tumbling out in their hurry to be heard. "For so long I've tried to find peace. I tried to blame my unhappiness on my mother-in-law. I thought that if I could only change her or wish her out of my life I would really be happy. I thought that the thing I wanted most was to have my husband and my home to myself—completely to myself.

"When I heard the words of the missionary on that first day we went to the Bible class, I thought how wonderful they sounded. But I still could not understand how we could love someone who does not return our love. Remember the things we talked of that day? You said that you thought Christianity taught good things, but that it was hard to be that good."

She paused to set her dishes on the ledge that ran around the sink, then said dreamily, "I thought as you did, but I wanted to try to use some of the teachings of Christianity in my life. I knew that I never could really love my mother-in-law, but I thought that perhaps if I tried to be more kind to her, she might be kinder to me. But it didn't work out that way."

"But Sachiko San, no one could really love a person like your mother-in-law! I . . ."

"No, let me finish, Matsuoka San! There is so much I must say." She stopped abruptly, and for just a moment she endured again the days of terror and the nights of weeping which had been her life since her marriage. "I tried to be kind," she continued more softly, "but every day I found myself hating more. I knew it infuriated her when I spent time with my husband, but I didn't pay any attention. I even felt a little superior because I had succeeded in winning him away from her. The only real reason I was kind to her at all was for my own benefit. I didn't want to be sent away, even though I wasn't happy in my husband's home. And I certainly didn't want the neighbors to talk about me. I was as wrong as she was. I know it now!"

Her eyes grew thoughtful and a little sad. She remembered the times when she had lived only to receive appreciation and love from her husband and in the end had failed in her reason for living. The bells of *Joya* came back to her, and with the sound of the bells came the despair of that midnight when life had seemed worse than death. She turned to her friend and said earnestly, "The time of real change in my life came when I realized that I was trying by my own power to do the impossible. I was trying to be kind by merely practicing rules and habits, but I had no real desire to be kind. It was something entirely external. I really had not changed at all. It was as if I had added a picture of Christ to the *butsudan* and intended to continue worshiping both him and the Buddha together. Have you ever seen that sort of thing in someone's home? I have.

"I talked to Roberts Sensei this morning, and all that she has taught us during the past two years came to a focus in my mind. I don't understand everything yet. In fact, I don't understand very much of anything. But when I talked to her, I realized suddenly that I did believe that God is. I knew that I needed something in my life—something I have been seeking for since I began to realize my own inability to live a good life. And I knew that God could help me to become a better person. I knew that he would help me to find peace."

She became suddenly self-conscious, glanced at Matsuoka and then down at her hands. Have I really talked so much? she wondered. What must she think of me? She moved to step into the kitchen and then stopped abruptly. Whatever she thinks, I can tell by her face that she doesn't understand. She doesn't believe what I do, she thought, almost in despair. How can I make her understand what I feel?

Matsuoka nodded politely, but her eyes were vague and preoccupied. "Well, if that's what you want, I'm glad you've found something that will help you."

"But I am a Christian!" Sachiko cried, as if by her crying she would be able to break down the wall which had arisen between them. "It's not just something I've adopted and added to my life. My love for Christ has become my meaning for living. I'm not the same person I was before!" But the wall remained there—it remained in the form of a peculiar blankness and reserve on the other woman's face. They were still friends, but their friendship was limited by Matsuoka's lack of understanding and belief.

"O God in heaven," Sachiko prayed, "is this part of it—the loneliness? Does it mean that I shall never feel close to my friends and family again? Does belief in You separate me from them in this way? If it does, give me strength to live without being understood." She turned her face to the inside of the house and the work which waited for her there.

Two hours later Sachiko stepped into the back seat of a taxi and waved good-by to her friend and the young high school girl who was to stay in the house while she was at the hospital. The back seat of the car was piled with *futon,* a teapot, a suitcase of her own clothes, and sleeping kimono for her mother-in-law.

"Are you sure you don't want me to go along?" Matsuoka called before the taxi pulled away from the curb. "I'll be glad to help."

"Thank you, Matsuoka San, but I think I shall be able to manage by myself." She smiled at the young girl. "Keiko Chan, *onegai shimasu!*"

"I'll do the best I can," Keiko answered shyly.

She is just a child, Sachiko thought to herself, but she

will be able to take care of Shiro and keep the dust off the furniture. Thieves won't break in if they know someone is staying there while we are gone.

As the taxi turned the corner, she looked back. They were still standing beside the path—Matsuoka's strong, vigorous figure slightly ahead of the girl's more slender form. Then the whole scene was swept from her, and she turned her eyes toward the street ahead.

"The women in the community are blaming you," Matsuoka had said casually, her arms full of *futon* and blankets. "They say that you should have stayed home to take care of your mother-in-law."

I knew that was what they would say, Sachiko said to herself, automatically clutching the seat in front of her as the taxi swerved around another car. If only I had thought before I ran away, but at the time it seemed the only thing to do. *Shikata ga nai!* It can't be helped now. She stretched her legs out in front of her. Then, wearily pushing aside a lock of hair which had fallen across her forehead, she lay her head back on the seat and closed her eyes. How terrible it must have been for her to be alone and ill! And Ichiro was sleeping in the next room but did not know that she needed him! I must make it up to her, she resolved. I'll do anything I can to help her to forget what took place last night!

The hospital was a large sprawling concrete building surrounded by a well-kept lawn with a pond. They drove through a gate that stood between the pillars of a high stone fence, circled the pond, and stopped before the wide entrance. A covered outdoor corridor led to other buildings—wooden buildings with windows decorated with towels and patients' laundry drying in the wind. Kimono-clad patients paced the corridors. Several stood watching the street from the entrance porch, while others walked among the brilliant azaleas and roses that bloomed beside the pond.

After the *futon* and suitcases had been deposited on the floor of the wide hall inside the main building, she paid the taxi driver and stepped out of her shoes and into straw slippers. Then she went to the desk to inquire the number of her mother-in-law's room.

She met Ichiro in the hall just outside the room.

"How is she?"

"She's better. Conscious now, and resting pretty well." He let himself down slowly onto the wooden bench that lined the hall. "I'm tired."

"You look tired. Is there anything I can do now?"

"There's not too much to do until she wakes up. Did you bring the things?"

"Yes, they are down in the lobby."

"Well, they will be all right there for a little while."

She sat down beside him, her eyes examining every line and angle of his face. She saw the weariness, the shock that had not yet faded from his eyes; it was the redness in them that reminded her of the preceding night. And she paused uneasily for a moment before she asked, "Can you tell me how she became ill?"

He only glanced at her face, but in that short time she knew that he had not forgotten what had happened. Her heart beat more quickly and she fought the trembling in her hands by clasping them strongly in her lap.

Ichiro rubbed his forehead, and when he answered his voice was even. "There's not much to tell." He stopped, then continued reluctantly, "I came home a little drunk and Mother had to let me into the house." He took a handkerchief from his pocket and wiped his face. "I overslept this morning and when I finally got up, I couldn't find anyone in the house at first. I opened the door to her room and there she was—lying on the floor." Perspiration appeared on his face again. He seemed unaware of it—did not seem to know even that she was beside him. "I can't tell you how horrible it was this morning—waking up and finding my mother unconscious. At first, I thought she was dead!"

"She will get better," she said, trying to keep her voice clear and strong.

The flush left his face. A thick mask of passivity settled down over it, making him a stranger to her again. "He's not going to say anything about my being gone last night," she said to herself, half-relieved, yet half-disappointed that he had not talked of it. She would have felt better if he had become angry and accused her of running away from him. She waited for him to speak, but when he did not, she turned from him and picked up her purse little self-consciously. "Well, I had better go and see about the *futon.*"

"I'll come along and help. Then we'll have to get back and see how she is."

Days in the hospital were almost all the same. The nights, too, followed a pattern. Sachiko learned to listen for the shallow breathing of her husband's mother. She learned to jump quickly from her bed when she was called, to make her way to the hallway for water, or to the desk beside the bed for a pill. She learned to adjust the *futon* comfortably over the older woman's shoulders. At times the sick woman could not sleep, and then Sachiko would sit for hours by her side, rubbing her back and shoulders and massaging her neck and legs. Day followed day and gradually, as the woman grew better, she became tired of the routine and dreariness of the hospital. Her tongue grew sharper, and her mind dwelt upon the things which had caused her to become bitter.

"This girl who is staying in the house while you are gone—are you sure you can trust her?" she asked one afternoon.

Sachiko looked up from her sewing. "Trust her?"

"Yes, trust her! Do you think you can?" The older woman's eyes watched her narrowly, slyly malevolent beneath heavy lids. Her skin during her sickness had turned sallow—almost paper-thin, and there was an odor of illness and decay about her that was almost overpowering.

"Why, yes. I believe I can trust her." Sachiko answered slowly, carefully.

"I think you are foolish to trust any young girl."

"But you know the Tanaka family. They are our nicest neighbors. I'm sure she is honest."

"Honest, yes. I didn't mean that."

The girl said nothing. Avoiding the piercing glance of her mother-in-law, she lowered her eyes to the stocking she held in her hand.

"What about your husband—do you trust him with a young girl in the house?" Hardly waiting for an answer, she continued harshly, "I wouldn't trust any man, especially a young man like Ichiro, in a house alone with another woman. Do you think he cares for you enough to be uninterested in any other woman? Anyone who believes that sort of thing is a fool! Where do you think he was the night you ran away from home? Drinking with the boys?" She laughed mockingly. "You tried so hard to turn him from me. Now, things have changed!" She stopped, but the sound of her hoarse breathing echoed through the silent room.

"Where did you go?"

"Go?" Here it comes, thought Sachiko. God, help me not to be afraid! She lay down the sewing and walked to the window, hiding her trembling hands with her body. She was surprised when she was able to echo quite calmly, "Where did I go?"

"Where did you go the night Ichiro came home late?" It was the hoarse, impatient cry of a hawk about to swoop down on its prey.

"I went to visit a friend."

"I wish I had time to visit friends of mine, especially when I have work in my own home to do. Did you have a nice ride on the train?" she asked curiously, slyly.

Sachiko was silent. She pressed her lips firmly together to avoid crying and turned her head once more to the window.

When she did not answer, the old woman sighed pettishly, "This is a boring, tiresome place to spend one's old age." She moved restlessly on the bed. "Come, cover me up, Sachiko. And get me another pill! If I can't get someone to talk to me, I might as well sleep."

When her husband's mother had finally fallen asleep, Sachiko took her Bible and slipped out of the room. She sat on the bench in the hall just outside the room and began to read. The walls of the hospital faded away. Once more it seemed that she sat in the missionary's house and heard the foreign woman say, "God loves you, Suzuki San. And as you read your Bible and pray to him, you will soon know that you love him, too. You will be able to stand any difficulty because your heavenly Father will give you strength to bear it with love in your heart."

The hall stretched out dark and bleak with rooms opening out on either side. She felt suddenly alone—terribly alone. It was an unusually quiet time of the day. No one walked the halls except for an occasional nurse or a patient marking time slowly up and down, up and down. Inside the room just opposite where she sat, the old woman dreamed of her son and waited longingly for the time he would come to visit her. She reserved her hatred and spite for the daughter-in-law who cared for her.

The girl's lips moved slowly as she read. "Lo, I am with you always, even unto the end of the world."[4] She was conscious that the Presence of Someone greater than herself sat beside her on the bench and continued to walk with her in the hospital.

[4]Matthew 28:20

CHAPTER THIRTEEN

THE DAMPNESS OF THE EARLY summer rains crept along the dark halls of the hospital, permeating every crack and corner of every room. Patients complained more often, tempers grew short, and *futon* and clothing began to smell with the musty odor of mildew and mold.

I hope Keiko Chan is taking care of Ichiro's shoes, Sachiko thought nostalgically one day. The clothes should be aired and bedding changed often, but she will probably not think of it. I'll have to remember to mention it to Ichiro. She listened to the rain falling on the roof of the corridor below her window. It beat upon the roses in the garden and, one by one, drenched and faded, the petals fell to the ground.

In the room behind her, her mother-in-law complained and muttered to herself. The rain and the querulous old woman—they had been a part of her for so long that she had learned to let them fall unheeded on her ears. But finally the muttering became so insistent that she could ignore it no longer. Turning reluctantly from the window, she cried with unusual emphasis, "But, *Okaasan,* it's raining now. Can't I wait until it stops?"

"Stops, nothing! It won't stop until July 10, and I can't wait that long for writing paper. It won't take you long to walk downtown and buy it for me."

Knowing that arguing would do no good, Sachiko put on her raincoat and taking her umbrella, started down the hallway to the first floor. She hesitated slightly before stepping out into the rain and thought of calling a taxi, but after fingering the few bills that still remained in her purse, she decided to walk.

Once she was actually walking in the rain, she began to enjoy it. Her feet, thrust into white boots and unencumbered by shoes, felt as if she were walking in the water barefoot. She breathed deeply and freely, and the rain that fell on her umbrella and coat enclosed her in a private world that belonged to her alone.

There were no sidewalks on the paved street leading from the hospital to the town. From time to time she stepped aside and using the umbrella to shield her clothing from the splashing water, waited for a three-wheeled truck or a taxi to pass. The leaves of the trees were the color of emeralds, the vegetation thick and lush. Hedges needing haircuts lined the road, countless little tips of growing branches marched along the top where they had been once sedately trimmed.

She stopped to let a group of children pass. Kindergarten children of three, four, and five years of age, their identical little fat legs trotted beneath identical raincoats and umbrellas. She watched them, red umbrellas for the girls and black ones for the boys, and wondered about the child she was never to have. She could hear them chattering excitedly with their teacher. Soon they would hurry into their respective *genkans* calling, "*Tadaima,*" and from somewhere in the house the mother would joyfully answer, *"Okaeri nasai,"* just as mothers had done every day of every year. And they would talk about their day in school. The mother would open the lunch box to find proudly that all the rice had been eaten. Handwork would be examined and notes from the teachers read.

A child to love and care for—how wonderful that would be! But then, the impossible always seems wonderful, she thought, trying deliberately to brush aside the scene that had intruded itself upon her mind. But in spite of all that she could do to forget it, the picture persisted until she could almost see the child, a baby with a red, red face.

Sometimes we could go places together, she dreamed, Ichiro and the baby and I. I would carry it on my back and keep it covered with a beautiful knitted blanket. When Ichiro came home at night, he would play with the child in the garden or walk with it beside the road. The child would sleep with us in our room until he became old enough to sleep by himself.

She dreamed, but not for long. Suddenly the realization that this dream could never come true became so strong that she felt nauseated. "I can never have a child," she cried to herself. And all the while the rain continued to beat down on her umbrella and cry with her, "Never a child . . . never a child . . . never a child . . ."

Yet out of that walk in the rain a thought was born. It continued to grow. Surely, somewhere in the world there would be a child that could belong to her. A child, perhaps, who had already made its way into this world —a child without parents to love it.

"But I could!" she cried out loud. "I could love someone else's child and accept it as my own!" A workman stepped aside to let her pass. He looked at her curiously, but she was not even aware that he was there, for her eyes were blinded by tears. "Oh, dear God! To have a child to care for and to teach! If I could have just one child, I would be forever thankful and happy." Inside, she was crying, desperately pleading. "I could love it and teach it to love You. I could . . ." Her body was full of unshed tears and she walked by herself, unaware that she had come to the highway and that across the street was the shopping area. It was only when she heard the policeman's warning whistle that she realized she was walking against a red light. Embarrassed, she turned and waited until the light had changed, then hurried into the stationery store.

She waited patiently that evening until Ichiro had talked with his mother and finally was ready to leave. She walked with him to the entrance, slipped on her boots and continued with him as far as the hospital gate. The rain had stopped falling, but the air was still damp. Her boots gasped and sighed with every step she took on the sodden grass.

She examined his face carefully while telling him of the thoughts she had had that afternoon. He stamped his feet on the ground several times, his face thoughtful and noncommittal.

"What do you think? Do you think we could . . .?"

"People don't usually adopt children from another family," he said slowly.

"But it wouldn't make any difference to me, Ichiro. Would it matter to you?"

"Well, you might not be sure just what kind of background the child had. Besides, I'm sure Mother wouldn't approve our adopting a stranger's child."

"But . . ."

"Wait!" he interrupted her. "There may be a possibility of something else."

It began to rain again, not in drops, but as a mist, softly caressing her face. She wiped it with her hands, her eyes clinging to his face as she did so.

"There may be the possibility of someone in the family. Not even a close relative, but some poor family who would consent to our raising a child and adopting it."

"Would your mother disapprove of that?" I hate to remind him of the power his mother has over us, she thought, but sooner or later we will have to ask her permission anyway.

"I don't know," he said, then paused. "But I think I'll write to the relatives in Kyushu and ask them whether they have any suggestions before I talk with her. They know she has been sick, and I don't think they will disturb her now. After we hear from them, we can talk with Mother. Perhaps if we can find a child from the family, she won't disapprove. She's concerned about our not having a child."

"I know."

He moved toward the gate. "I'll write tonight. We should know pretty soon whether it is possible or not."

"I hope it is possible."

He smiled at her. Suddenly, she loved him so much that it hurt. She thought, If we only had a real chance to know each other, how happy we would be! She smiled to herself. How proud I am of him! My husband!

Long after he had disappeared from sight, she stood by the gate in the rain, thinking of the things they had talked about, dreading the time when she must go in and climb the stairs to the second floor where a cantankerous old woman waited for her to do her bidding. "I hope it is possible," she said again, thoughtfully, hopefully. "I hope it is."

July was hot and damp. Once more the *futon* were loaded into the back of a taxi, and Sachiko and her mother-in-law returned home. For the first time the house felt like home to Sachiko. The veranda, opened to the sun, but shaded here and there by trees in the garden, made the house look clean and light. Summer flowers were blooming in the garden—gladioli and poppies—and the bamboo trees sang to her as the wind blew through their tall upper branches. She woke early in the mornings with a song on her lips and cleaned until the house seemed almost to sparkle.

Even her mother-in-law seemed pleased to be back in her own room and in her own home. Her tongue was not so bitter, and her eyes softened a little as she returned to the sewing she had left unfinished. But she stirred very little from her room. When she did leave it, she walked slowly and carefully. Suddenly, she seemed old beyond her years, and Sachiko felt pity well up in place of the hatred which had once dominated her life.

Ichiro came home early from school and spent time

with his mother in her room so that Sachiko very seldom saw him alone. But a certain amount of peace permeated the house, and for the first time there was a degree of closeness between the members of the family.

The day the letter came from Kyushu, Sachiko sat quietly massaging her mother-in-law's shoulders while her husband and the older woman talked of its contents. Outwardly she was calm, her face pleasantly controlled, and her hands gentle and strong. But her heart beat crazily and she waited impatiently, her whole being following every expression, every intonation of the voices of the two people who held within their hands the power to grant or to withhold from her the joy of having a child.

"But three years old! Certainly you don't want a child as old as that! Are you sure the Matsutake family won't give up their youngest baby? They have so many!"

"No. Uncle said that there was only this one child—this little boy."

"I had forgotten that the Mori family is related to our family—through the child's mother, wasn't it?" Yoshiko Suzuki reached for her glasses and examined the letter. " 'The father remarried and his new wife has children by a former husband,' " she read slowly. She glanced at Ichiro, her eyes narrowing slightly. "It's true that the child would be lost to the family if he were not adopted. His mother was the only tie to our family, and now that she is dead, there isn't too much to hold him." She paused for a moment and then continued slowly, "Well, perhaps we could try it, and if it works out we can adopt him later. If it doesn't, we can always send him back to his father."

"I should make preparations to go to Kyushu right away—as soon as school is out. But I can't stay long because I have to be back for some of the summer activities."

"Well, as long as you have to wait a week or so before you can go, you had better get reservations on the *Asakaze*. You have to buy your tickets a week ahead for third-class sleepers, so you'd better see about that tomorrow. School is out next Monday, isn't it?"

"Yes, Monday is the last day."

"Then plan to leave on Tuesday morning."

"I'll go check on the time tonight, and then if I can get tickets tomorrow, I'll take off from school to do it. We don't have to go to Tokyo for them anymore. We can get them at Tachikawa Station."

"That's good. It won't take so long, then."

How can they talk about such inane things when something so important is happening to us! Sachiko wondered as her hands continued to move rhythmically across her mother-in-law's body. A child! A child of my own! She forgot her dream of a baby, and suddenly it seemed that she had always wanted a boy child. A little boy with sparkling, wondering eyes. Trembling slightly with excitement, she finished kneading the older woman's neck and shoulders and covered her carefully. Strong anticipation remained with her as she planned for the child's coming.

What will he be like? she wondered day after day, as she waited for the time when the child would enter the house. Will he be a happy child? Or have the three years with his father taught him to fear instead of love? A dingy room, his mother's death, a stepmother with children of her own—at three years of age a child is still a baby, but even a baby knows when he is not loved.

Suddenly she felt desperate. Could she be a real mother to a child of whom she knew almost nothing? "Will he like us?" she asked herself. "Can I help him to forget the unhappiness he has known?" Will he like the city—a country child who is used to living where no one tries to keep him within certain limits? Will he want to return to his home? The questions echoed and re-echoed through her mind as she washed and cleaned her husband's clothes and packed the suitcase for the trip. They sang with the wheels of the train as it entered the station and continued to ring in her mind as her thoughts followed her husband to Tokyo and from there to the southernmost island of the country. The questions went with her when she returned to the silent house—silent except for the complainings of an old woman and the gentle murmurings of the bamboo trees. Will he love us? Shall we be able to help him? Can we . . . ?

She did not know that on the other side of the city, near the Base where the hum of the airplanes could be heard almost constantly, a young missionary woman prayed daily that Sachiko would grow, that she would find peace and happiness. Sachiko only knew that day after day she became more conscious of her increasing love for Christ.

On the train the young husband thought of his wife and wondered at his weakness in letting difficulties drive a wedge between them. He remembered the quietness and gentleness of her beauty and wished desperately that he knew how to make her happy. Finally, he rolled over and stretched his legs carefully in the cramped area of his Pullman. Then, turning off the light, he slept while the express train sped swiftly south to the country place where his new son waited for him.

And in Kyushu the boy who waited did not know why he cried often in the night. He knew that something warm had gone from his life, but he did not know that it was because his mother no longer lived. His father had older sons to whom he must give his life and a new young wife to please. Stiff and afraid, but rebellious because his mother had left him, the little one lay in his *futon* listening to the hoarse breathing of his stepbrothers. A train whistled in the night, but it had no meaning for him. He did not know nor could he have understood what a difference the coming of a train would make in his life. He only knew that he was lonely and that his father no longer cared.

CHAPTER FOURTEEN

THE CLICKING OF THE WHEELS lulled him half to sleep. Then the child's head fell heavily against him, and he reached his arm around the small thin body and held it firmly.

It was dark. Ichiro could see the people sleeping in the seat opposite his. They sat propped against each other like huge dolls, their bodies swaying with every movement of the train. Huddled mounds of other passengers filled the aisle. A crumpled newspaper, a wrapping from a tangerine package, or a coat spread on the floor served as a hard bed for those who had arrived too late to find a seat. The child grew heavy. Ichiro laid him gently down on the seat, making a pillow of his coat. The train lurched and suddenly all desire for sleep fled.

It's hot, he thought. He opened the window, but the smoke from the engine blew back in his face, and he shut it again. "If I don't get more air," he said to himself, "I shall not be able to breathe."

Another child cried, loudly and unrestrainedly. A woman's gentle voice soothed and hushed it, but it continued to cry with renewed anger. Beside Ichiro, the little boy stirred, opened his eyes and looked around him. Then reassured, he went back to sleep.

Ichiro had thought he would be able to get a ticket for the superexpress, but when he had inquired after arriving at Hakata Station, he had discovered that they were all sold. So there was no choice but to return by regular express. Fortunately, he and the boy had been able to get seats, but the train soon became uncomfortably crowded. Scenes from the past few hours flashed through his mind. The farmhouse where he had found the child, the father gone, and the stepmother anxious to be rid of him. The child's eyes had been wide with fear, but his thin little legs had followed Ichiro obediently. He remembered the Hakata train station where they had waved good-by to the aged relatives from Fukuoka City and where they had stood in line for hours before boarding the coach. They found a seat, covered with green velvet, the back vertical, uncomfortably fitted to a man's back.

At one of the stations he had bought boxes of rice balls for himself and the child and tiny earthen pots of hot tea. The voices of the venders of tangerines, candy, rice cookies, and box lunches mingled in a symphony, weird and nasal, some high-pitched and some carrying the melody in a low alto, while outside his window friends bowed and chattered to departing passengers. The child had eaten quickly and silently, as if he were afraid that the box might be snatched from him.

"Do you want tangerines?" Ichiro asked him, and the boy nodded quickly, turning his face toward the window. The train started again. Even as they started out of the station, a train coming from the opposite direction entered on the other track, and the cries of the venders could be heard again—*"I—su—cur—eemu . . .* ice cream . . ."

The world flashed by them, and the boy sat with his nose pressed against the window. A straw-thatched farmhouse; a new concrete school building; a torii guiding the way to a country shrine; two women and a girl dressed in baggy *mompe* pants with packs on their backs, walking up a mountain road; a clump of trees sheltering a cemetery—the stones and sticks rising out of the ground, giving it the cluttered appearance of a child's sandbox; kimono material, stretched tight on long boards, standing up against a house to dry; a town with tile roofs, and then the country again—they all seemed familiar but at the same time strange to Ichiro. He was eager for the noise and excitement of the city.

He looked down at the tousled head of the boy who sat beside him. What was he thinking, this child who so short a time before had left the only home he had ever known with a stranger whom he had never seen before? The child called Ichiro uncle, but this was only a polite name which any child gives to a man whose name he does not know or with whom he feels no particular relationship. What did he think when each second took him farther away from all that was familiar? He was only a three-year-old boy, but there was something old and wise about the way he avoided the eyes of the man who sat beside him.

He spoke only once and that was to ask, "When does this train get to Tokyo, *Ojiisan?*" Ichiro told him and he asked again, making it more of a statement than a question, "Then soon I will be able to go back to my home, won't I?"

"We want you to visit us for a while, Shinobu Chan," Ichiro said somewhat uncomfortably. And the child turned toward the window again, seemingly satisfied with the indirect answer.

They would arrive in Tokyo in the morning, about twenty-four hours after leaving Kyushu. Twenty-four hours of hot, fetid air in a crowded coach. Twenty-four hours of sitting cramped in a seat while under one's feet-tangerine skins and papers mingled with the unwanted magazines of careless passengers. Ichiro stretched his legs and as he moved he woke the child, who began to cry, tears filling his eyes and flooding his cheeks. He offered no resistance, but all of the loneliness of the past year, all of the pain of being shoved aside for a younger, more lovable stepbrother, the bewilderment of being taken from his home—all of these stood in the child's face and were a part of the sobs that shook his narrow shoulders.

Ichiro picked him up and cradled him in his arms. The child clung to him as gradually the crying ceased and only the stain of tears remained on his face and a slight hiccup shook his chest. He slept again, his head pressed against Ichiro's shoulder. The man's face rested on the boy's black hair, and gradually he slept, too. He woke only when the sun finally had set the mountains on fire with radiant morning light.

Sachiko opened the closet door and reaching to the highest shelf, pulled down the new *futon* which had been bought for the child. It fell about her, heavy but clean-smelling, its brilliant colors yet unfaded by the sun. She held it to her, felt its softness against her face and stood for a moment enveloped in the newness of it, her eyes closed.

He had come through the gate with Ichiro, his eyes coolly impersonal and averted from the old woman's sharp black ones and Sachiko's warmly loving ones. His thin legs looked pathetically childlike beneath the short pants he wore, and his face was grimy from the dirt of the train. He had looked with polite indifference at each of the things Ichiro had shown him—the garden, the house. In only two things had he shown interest. A plane had flown over the house headed for the Base. It was so low that they could see the pilot and the markings on the side. Shinobu had stood for a long time watching it, then had run about the garden excitedly, a miniature pilot on an imaginary plane. And for just a moment when he saw Shiro, he had stopped and buried his face in the dog's wiggling soft neck. Then he had left the dog, his interest of the moment seemingly gone.

Vainly Sachiko had tried to interest him in a book, a ball—anything, but he had shown no interest in her. Indeed, he seemed to avoid the women of the house. She smiled, remembering how he had followed Ichiro about all day to the public baths, to the department store, and to the gate for the mail.

"He was worried," she said to herself. "He was worried that Ichiro would leave him." Will he ever forget? she wondered. Will he forget that he was not loved and will he now be able to accept and give love? How can you teach a child to love when he has no concept of its meaning? "Oh, God," she cried, "how could they take out their frustrations on a child who cannot fight back and defend himself?"

She was held back by reserve—a feeling of not wanting to frighten the child by her own feelings. So on that first day in their home, she had waited for him to find himself in his new surroundings. She had waited for him to approach her first.

"Sachiko!" Her mother-in-law's voice came from just outside her door. "Would you make up a bed for Shinobu Chan? I'm going to bed early tonight, and I think he should go to bed now, too. He was up traveling all last night."

"Yes, *Okaasan.*" She began to spread the *futon* on the floor beside her own.

"Oh, not here!" the older woman continued, peering into the room. "Put it in my room. I'll take care of him."

The blood drained from Sachiko's face. Suddenly she understood the meaning of her mother-in-law's words only too well. Her fingers trembled as she continued smoothing the *futon* on the floor, while her mind sought frantically for words which would not hurt but which would express the things she felt. Is he not to be my child after all? she asked herself almost desperately. Am I not to be his mother?

"Did you hear me?" her husband's mother said again, grasping the corner of the new *futon.* "Let's put it in my room."

Sachiko let it drop to the floor and with her hands clasped in front of her, turned to face the other woman. "*Okaasan,* you need all the rest you can get," she began softly. "If the child cries in the night, it would not be good for you to get up to take care of his needs."

"The child won't give me any trouble."

"I think it would be best for him to sleep here so that

if he cries, it will not disturb you." For the first time, Sachiko looked directly at the older woman.

"Who are you to say what you feel is best!" Her face flushed with anger. "Do you think you have any rights in this house? Is this your child, born to you? If you could have given Ichiro a child, do you think we would have sent to poor relations for a makeshift child? It is because of you that we have to swallow our pride and consent to such an arrangement! And now you want to pretend that he belongs to you. I'll tell you something! If you are going to get such strong thoughts in your mind, we'll send him home on the next train! We'll . . ."

"Mother!" Ichiro stood in the entrance. "You'll make yourself ill!"

Sachiko said nothing, but before she turned to close the closet door, she caught a glimpse of wide eyes in a small face, a little body that shrank against her husband and a mouth that was contorted with fear. Her heart stopped for a moment and then, heavily, painfully beat on. But inside, she cried for the child who had once again been hurt.

Yoshiko Suzuki turned and went into her room. Sachiko realized that the victory had been her own. But she shuddered as she thought of the possible results of that victory. The child is turned against me already, she thought as she finished making his bed. I shall have to be very patient.

When she had finished, she went out to the veranda to find him. He was sitting on the edge, his feet clad in her husband's large *geta* and hanging over the side, his eyes fixed on the lights of an airplane which was fast disappearing into the darkness.

"Shinobu Chan," she said softly and sat down beside him. But he sprang to his feet and ran out into the garden and hid behind a tree. It was only after she had called Ichiro and he had coaxed him into the house that he would consent to come to bed. Even then, he would not let her undress him nor could she wash his face. His body stiff, his breath loud in the quietness of the room, he lay for a long time without sleeping.

Time after time during the long night that followed, she rose to lift him gently back into his bed from which he had crawled. Each time his body jerked or twisted, and each time he cried or murmured in his sleep, she woke trembling. Finally, she eased him into her own bed and lay awake with him cradled within the curve of her arm the rest of the night. When the first sign of day filtered its way through the heavy *amado* shutters, she fell asleep. The child's body relaxed and the tension fled.

That morning the same sweet innocence which rested on the little boy's face could also be found on the face of the young woman. Rebelliousness and fear were gone. For just a moment, peace and trust flowed between them, unconscious but real. It was a beginning, a promise of the love which was to grow.

Sachiko slipped her arm out from beneath the child carefully so that she would not wake him, dressed quietly, and then started to the kitchen to begin the breakfast. On the way through the darkened house, she picked up his ball and the book which had dropped to the floor unused the night before.

What a change a child makes in a house, she thought. It has a different feeling, a happier feeling. She stood outside the kitchen door for a minute breathing the freshness of the morning air. "I'll get the work done quickly and then I can spend the rest of the day with Shinobu Chan," she said to herself as she washed the rice. She drained the water from the pan and after carefully measuring the proper amount for cooking, added it to the rice. Ichiro will not be able to stay home today, her thoughts ran, and so I shall have to be free to take care of him. She placed the lid on the pan, carried it into the kitchen, and lit the fire.

Shinobu slept late that morning. Long after Ichiro had left for work at the school, long after the older woman had eaten her breakfast and combed her long hair, pinning it into a bun on the top of her head, long after Sachiko had washed the clothes and hung them out in the sun to dry he slept, his arm thrown out above his head. Sachiko came in to look at him time after time. Once she pulled the *futon* up over his shoulder. Another time she wiped the perspiration from his face. Each time she saw him, she knew that she was learning to love him as she would have loved her own child.

She was sweeping the garden when the silence of the morning was pierced by the child's screams of terror. Dropping the broom, she ran to the house. She met her mother-in-law in the eating room, and stepping hastily ahead of her, knelt by his bed.

"Sachiko, let me take him," the older woman said, trying to push her way in front of the girl. "You've had no experience with anything like this."

Sachiko pretended that she did not hear, picked up Shinobu and carried him to the open veranda. She sat there in the morning sun for a long time until the trembling in his body had died away.

"It was only a bad dream," she said to him softly over and over. "You will be all right. It was only a dream. Now, see? It's gone, isn't it?" For the moment, her awareness of the child's need of her was more powerful than her fear of her mother-in-law's anger. Even as she held the child in her arms, she knew that after today the hatred of the older woman would grow; she also realized that she was powerless to prevent it from doing so.

The dog barked once, then began to whine. The child smiled suddenly through his tears. "Shiro!" he called. He looked at Sachiko and laughed, and the dream was forgotten. Forgotten, that is, until it would come again, and again, and then would gradually stop coming altogether.

"Let's eat our breakfast first," she said. "Then you can go outside and play with the dog."

He ate quickly but noisily, eager to be done with it. His manners, like his country speech, are terrible, she thought fondly. But then, we will help to change that after a while if we are patient. When he had finished, they went out into the garden together.

"I had a dog like this, *Obaasan,*" he said, laughing while trying to avoid Shiro's frantic tongue. "It was a little white dog, all white, and I called him Chebie."

"We're glad Shiro has someone to play with now. He was lonesome for a boy. He is glad you came to visit us," she answered, deliberately using the word "visit" until such a time when she would feel that he really wanted to stay.

"Yes," he looked seriously up at her. "I have to go home tomorrow."

Tomorrow! Tomorrow he would not go home. But she knew that to him tomorrow did not mean what it meant to her. Tomorrow meant sometime, next week, this week, next month, or when he wanted something to happen.

"Yes," she said aloud, knowing all the time that he would not go home and that soon he would almost forget the terror of not being wanted in the house in Kyushu. "Yes," she said again. But she said it only to keep him from feeling afraid and to assure him that he did, to some extent, have some control over his own life.

"You make me think of someone," he said thoughtfully, wrinkling his forehead.

"Your stepmother?"

"Oh, no! You're not like her at all! You remind me of someone I knew once."

"Really?"

"Umn-hmn." He fingered the dog's ears absently. "We lived on a farm near Fukuoka. Do you know where Fukuoka is?"

"Yes, I know, but I've never been there."

"It's a long way from here. We came on the train, the

man and I." He looked into the house. "Where is the man—*Ojiisan?*"

"He had to go to school today."

"Does he go to school?"

"Yes, he is a teacher."

He was silent. "Oh, then he has to go to school every day?"

"Yes."

"But he will come back again?"

"Yes, he'll come home this afternoon."

He paused, considering, then smiled up at her. "I like *Ojiisan.*" His eyes narrowed. "Do you know my father?"

"No, I don't."

"I don't like my father!"

Hiding the shock and pity she felt, she answered, "Don't you like him?"

"Well, I used to, but not anymore." He averted his face, but his voice faltered.

"Would you like to help me get the mail?" she said swiftly, forcing herself to speak.

"Hai!" And he was off to the gate.

"Sachiko!" Her mother-in-law stood in the entranceway. Sachiko turned back toward the house, leaving the child to run on by himself. "Don't you think you had better do your work?" Her face stiff and her eyes cold, she stood above Sachiko on the hall floor. Suddenly she seemed very tall and powerful, making Sachiko feel young and unsure of herself. "Send the child in to me," the older woman demanded. "I'll take care of him. There is shopping and other work which you can do."

The child stood beside Sachiko, his head pressed against her arm. "Shopping? Can I go, too?"

The other woman turned with a faintly triumphant look on her face. "No, Shinobu Chan. I need a big boy to help me with my yarn. Come quickly."

Sachiko stood silently in the doorway. Even though the sun was hot on her back, she shivered suddenly as if a cold wind had blown across her body.

CHAPTER FIFTEEN

SACHIKO WIPED THE PERSPIRATION from her forehead and adjusted the parasol so that the sun did not strike her face. It was already hot and humid, and the day promised to become even more unbearable. "Ask the teacher if Shinobu Chan can enter kindergarten this fall, Sachiko," her mother-in-law had said. "He will soon be four, and since he hasn't had proper training until he came here, it would be best for him to enter kindergarten as soon as possible."

She paused beside the missionary's gate and watched the children playing in a portable rubber wading pool which had been borrowed for the summer play week. She smiled as she saw the smaller children of the kindergarten start bravely across the pool, then stop to catch their breath. Their hair plastered to their heads, bodies sleek and tanned, they fought for the balls and plastic toys that dotted the surface of the water. A little girl with fat braids and a red swimming suit ducked her head experimentally and then wiped her eyes before cautiously submerging again.

"Tanoshisoo desu ne!"

The missionary stood behind her, her eyes narrowed against the glare of the morning sun, her face wrinkled with laughter.

"It must be wonderful to be a child and be so happy," Sachiko agreed pensively. "To have no worries, to be unconcerned about what other people think, to think only of exciting things to do and learn! What would it be like to be a child again?"

"Yes, but doing as you want doesn't always bring happiness, does it? Even for a child?"

Sachiko nodded slowly. "A child who has had nothing and then receives everything he asks for certainly is not a happy child. And yet it is the Japanese way to give children as much happiness and freedom as they desire." She paused and went on thoughtfully. "We believe that childhood must be a happy time for children. Then, as the child grows older, more will be required of him, and he will need stricter supervision." She glanced swiftly at the other woman. "That is one way in which the Japanese way of doing things is different from the American way." The laughter of the children seemed very far away. Even after she had stopped speaking, she was aware only of the eyes of the American woman. They were warm and held a deep willingness to understand. Sachiko looked down at the shopping basket she held on her arm. "It's hard to know what is best to do."

The heat of the sun beat down upon them. "Come into the house," Emile Roberts said gravely. "It's warm out here, too warm to stand in the sun very long."

"I have to return home soon."

"Then come in for only as long as you can stay. It has been a long time since we've been able to talk very much."

The *tatami*-mat room was cool and comfortable. Sachiko knelt on a cushion, sipped slowly the glass of cold juice the missionary brought her, and felt immediately refreshed.

"And yet," Emile continued after she had served them, "is a child happy when there are no limits as to what he can demand? When he does not know what behavior is expected of him?" It was the same question she had asked previously; it was only phrased in a different way.

"He is not really happy, is he?" Sachiko answered hesitantly. She was silent for a moment.

"You have a little boy in your home, now?"

Sachiko smiled. Warmth spread through her body as

she remembered her child. "Yes, he has lived with us for three weeks."

"I heard about it just the other day."

"We are so happy with him."

"You were lonesome before, weren't you?"

"Yes, a woman without a child in Japan is usually very lonesome." Sachiko paused. "However, things are still not as they should be. It is difficult to raise a child when one's mother-in-law has such different ideas about ways of doing things."

The missionary woman looked intently at her hands lying folded in her lap. "I'm sure it must be difficult." Then she raised her eyes to Sachiko's face and said gently, "Are you happy now, Suzuki San?"

"Yes, I am happy. My life was changed after I made the decision I did the night I came to talk with you. I don't mean to say that things are easier. In some ways things are easier since Shinobu came, but in other ways it has become more difficult. Yet, I am happy and I know that I have peace in my heart. I feel that Christ is helping me to become a stronger person. I pray every day that he will make me strong."

"It would be good if you could come to church. You need to know other Christians."

"I know. I think that soon I may be able to begin coming on Sunday mornings." She stopped, sat for a moment phrasing her thoughts, and then continued, "Shinobu grew up in the country and we are very anxious for him to learn better habits and a more polite way of talking. I'm sure it will be an inconvenience, but we wondered if there is any possibility that he may be able to enter the kindergarten this fall? We thought of waiting until spring when the new term begins, but have begun to think that, if at all possible, it would be better for him to enter at once. Do you suppose he could be allowed to attend this fall?"

"Let me ask the principal of the school. He would be able to tell you more definitely than I could. Sometimes children drop out of school, and if that has happened, there would probably be a place for Shinobu Chan. I hope there is, for we would be happy for him to come."

"I can go over to the church and ask. There is no need for you to trouble yourself."

"No, really, I would like to go with you." They rose and moved to the entrance, put on their shoes, and walked out into the brilliance of the August morning. Dust on the playground rose up around their feet in little puffs while the hot breeze continued to swing the tiny glass chimes of the *furin* in the neighbor's veranda. And from the open windows of the church building came the sound of children's voices singing joyously, sweetly.

The green ears of the rice finally dropped their heads and turned a golden brown. Then in the rice fields surrounding the city, the swish of sickles and the rhythmic swaying of the farmers' bodies, together with the sound of the threshing machines, proclaimed the news that fall had come. The locusts sang in the trees amid the lingering heat. Every day, after returning from kindergarten, Shinobu would take his net attached to a long pole and leave the house. His family would not see him again until he returned just before dinner with a boxful of insects. Sachiko would glance out the front door or through the open veranda to catch a glimpse of his long bare legs beneath short pants. She would watch him bending down to look intently at the ground or lifting his head to look at the trees. Then with a tender smile on her face, she would return to her work. She found little time now to think of herself. More and more her life and thoughts centered about the desires and actions of Shinobu.

Every morning she would dress him in his blue hat and blue cotton uniform, place his lunch box packed full of rice or sandwiches in his bag, and putting it over his shoulder, would walk with him to school. They passed the fish market long before the day's load of fish had arrived. The bare shelves in the window of the shop made it look deserted and shabby. They bowed lightly as they returned the greetings of the bread and cooky shopkeeper, avoided the bicycles that carried high school students to school or businessmen to work. Sometimes they stepped aside for a bicycle taking a family of three for an outing. The baby's head always bobbed freely on its mother's back, its black eyes sparkling.

Sometimes Shinobu would run ahead or would stop to pet a dog or to watch a cat cross the road before them, its short tail held aloft with dignified disdain. Then Sachiko would walk on alone, knowing that he would soon come running to catch up with her, grasp her hand, and ask innumerable questions, all beginning with "Why" or "What."

When they would draw near the church, he would pull away from her and run excitedly toward the door, calling all the time in a loud voice, *"Ohayo, Sensei."* Without fail, from the inside of the church building or from outside near the swings the teacher would answer, *"Ohayo gozaimasu,* Shinobu Chan!" Sachiko would watch him, suddenly strangely saddened that he left her side so gladly—yet happy that he loved the kindergarten and the Christian teachers who taught him every day.

Sometimes she would talk to the missionary, usually outside the gate. Then she would return to her house, her feet swift and light, and her heart would sing the whole day as she wondered, amazed, at the joy she had found since she had become a Christian. She was glad that her son was learning to sing, to read simple Japanese symbols and characters, to write his name. Also he was hearing the stories which are a part of Japanese folklore.

Most of all, she was happy when he returned to say, "*Sensei* told us a story about Jesus today," or, "We take turns when we use the swings at kindergarten," or again, "God made the flowers, Mother. *Sensei* told me so." And she would echo within her heart, "I will sing unto the Lord, because he hath dealt bountifully with me."[1]

He had been attending kindergarten only one month when he began insisting vehemently before every meal that they must pray before eating. When he first suggested it, his father had smiled indulgently. "All right, Shinobu. Show us how you pray in kindergarten."

"No. You pray, *Otoosan,*" he had replied, suddenly aware that their eyes were all fixed on him.

"Your father doesn't know how to pray," his grandmother said wryly. "I've tried to get him to go to the temple with me many a time, but so far the only time he will go is at New Year's holidays."

"Mother knows how to pray."

The older woman became silent, but bitterness filled her eyes. She glanced meaningfully at her son, but when he flushed, turning his face from her to the food before him, she rose and went to the kitchen. The door slammed shut behind her.

"Mother, please pray," Shinobu insisted innocently. "It's your turn first."

A pot banged in the kitchen and the outer door closed. Sachiko shuddered, avoiding the eyes of her young husband. Then, when the silence had continued for too long, seeing the pleading face of the child before her, she began quietly to pray. *"Mainichi no tabemono ni tsuite, fukaku kansha itashimasu."* "Thank you for the food," her lips said, but her heart cried, "Help me not to be afraid." Her voice faltered only once, then, as if strengthened by a power outside her own, it grew clear and resonant.

In the kitchen the older woman listened, her face still and her breath coming short. *Ten no Otoosama . . .* heavenly Father! She laughed. "Father, indeed!" She

---

[1]Psalm 13:6

laughed, but it was uneasy laughter, and she was filled with a premonition of strange things to come.

The bitterness grew and grew, gathered strength and soon permeated every area of their life in the home. The evil which had taken root long before was arrested when the child first came, but now was a raging monster. It choked out all freedom and warmth and made them afraid to trust. The child soon learned not to mention his mother or her beliefs. The word "Christian" was not used often. When it was, it was spat out angrily from the older woman's lips, and the name of the daughter-in-law was always connected with it.

But in spite of the hate which spread from the old woman to all parts of the household, Sachiko continued to walk about the house with peace in her eyes. If she wept, it was only when she knew that no one was in the house to hear her. The child, perhaps because he had learned to do so in his kindergarten, continued to pray before his meals, but he no longer suggested that his mother do it.

Every Sunday morning, whether it was raining or clear, after Shinobu had returned from Sunday school with his kindergarten class at the church, Sachiko left for the church service. When she had first asked to go, she had expected that never would her husband's mother give her permission, but as Sunday after Sunday went by and still she was allowed to leave, she did not question the reasons. She was thankful that nothing was done to hinder her going.

Quietness always came over her when she entered the door of the church, took off her shoes in the large *genkan,* and slid her feet into slippers provided by the church. Somehow her feeling of worship also was associated with her son, for it was here he worshiped and played during the mornings and early afternoons of almost every day of the week. She shared with him love for the church and for the worship of the church. It was a bond that tied them closer together than she had dared dream would be possible.

She opened the door to the sanctuary, walked in silently, her hymnal and Bible in her hands, slipped into a seat near the back and bowed her head to pray. Each Sunday it was the same. The ritual became a part of her and was even so a part also of that which was holy and strengthening and peaceful. Her feet held closely together and flat on the floor, her hands clasped in her lap, she prayed as one filled with awe but also as a person intimately acquainted with her God. She stood when she sang, sat down when she prayed. When the minister bowed lightly before speaking, she also bowed with the rest of the congregation in response, a mere dip of the head and shoulders. It was a symbol of the respect she felt for him as a man of God and as her leader.

She was conscious of God and of her need to grow. She felt an especially close relationship between herself and the other Christians who gathered together every Sunday morning to worship. The quietness held them together; it also sent them out stronger and better able to face their own particular Calvarys, their own individual struggles.

Sachiko grew, but was not conscious that she was growing. She did not know that her daily walk brought her closer to God and that she was finding maturity as a child learns to take steps. She only knew that she fell often. She was conscious of her mistakes, of her inability to smile always, no matter what was said about her in her home, of her impatience when her husband failed to return until late at night and then always with the smell of sake on his clothing.

But she did know that, in spite of these burdens, she was no longer dissatisfied or unhappy. She wept, but had no sense of loneliness or despair. The smile came easily to her lips even when the tears had only a moment before fled from her eyes. She did not know that she grew, but the missionary woman knew. Emile Roberts watched her growing, and the warmth that had lain between them also continued to grow.

A typhoon came the last of September, and the child cried in the night. At first a weak, whimpering cry, it rose with the wind to a scream of terror. Sachiko held him. She tried with her love to take his attention from the swaying and whirling of the world outside their window, but for this one time her love was not enough, and he continued to cry, his hand clutching her kimono. A big tree in the garden blew down, narrowly missing the house. She heard the bathroom chimney fall and go skittering across the yard. Then there was only the sound of the wind, a screaming, frenzied wind, gone suddenly crazy, bent on destroying everything in its path. She heard the rain and knew that in spite of the preparations they had made after listening to the storm warnings on the radio, the water was coming into the house. It seeped in from under the window sills and through the broken tiles on the roof.

"What time is it, Sachiko?" Her husband woke, shifted his body so that he could see out the window.

"I don't know—the electricity is off. About three or three-thirty, I think."

"Won't he sleep?"

"I don't think so."

"Take him in your bed. It shouldn't last more than two hours or so longer."

She lifted the *futon* and laid the child inside, then slipped in beside him, holding him close to her. The house rocked again and he screamed.

"Shinobu," she said, "Mother and Father are here with you. You don't have to be afraid." He continued to whimper, his body stiff and tense. "Remember the things your teacher has told you in kindergarten? That God takes care of you during the night? God loves you. We are always safe with him." She talked to the child, but even as she did it, she knew that she was also trying to reassure herself. It was as if, by talking, she could help herself to believe that they were safe, that the wind would go away, and the moon and stars come out. When the wind grew stronger, she sang. She sang every song she knew, songs Shinobu had learned in the Sunday school and kindergarten, hymns about God's care.

In the lull of the storm, she heard her mother-in-law's voice calling. She started up, ready to go to her, when the words she was saying became sentences, and understanding, Sachiko knew that it would do no good to talk.

"Don't teach the child that stuff! Stop making so much noise and go to sleep."

Sachiko slid back between the mattresses and held the boy close to her again. He snuggled against her, and she felt the tears start in her throat. Beside her Ichiro stirred, then leaned over her.

"He's sleeping now. You'll be tired tomorrow, so you had better try to sleep." He said it almost tenderly and for just a moment his hand brushed her cheek.

The three of them together in this room, a family pitting their strength against the wind and the storm—a warm feeling welled up within her, and worry left her. Peace took its place and she slept.

When she woke it was day and the wind was gone. A beautiful day. If it had not been for the tree which lay across the walkway, or the tiles which covered the ground, she would have thought of the night before as only a dream. Suddenly lighthearted, she began to repair the damage the wind had brought. In her heart she sang the same song of thankfulness the sparkling morning sang. The peace of the morning echoed the great peace that filled her whole being.

CHAPTER SIXTEEN

"SACHIKO SAN," Kawaguchi San said cheerfully, "I've been trying to persuade your mother to come and stay with me for a couple of days. Can't you talk her into it?"

Yoshiko Suzuki smiled self-consciously. "It's too late for an old woman like me to start leaving home. When it comes time for me to die, I want to die at home."

Her friend laughed a trifle too loudly. "Old woman? Why, if you are old, I certainly must be ready for the grave right now. You're not older than I am, Suzuki San!" Her tongue lied, but her eyes did not. Pity flashed across them for a moment as she saw the stoop that had come into the older woman's shoulders during the last year. She turned to the girl. "Can't you get along without *Okaasan* for a week or so? It's time she had a good vacation."

Sachiko said nothing. If I should say yes, she would never leave this house, she thought uncomfortably. But if I should say no, she might feel that she must stay. She knew, however, that what she thought was not really important to them. So she smiled and bowed slightly in answer to the question.

For a long time Mrs. Kawaguchi had not come to visit them. But then, during the last month, her gushingly polite voice had often been heard coming from the guest room where the two women would sit by the hour laughing and talking.

I've never been able to stand the woman, thought Sachiko. But somehow, it is even more difficult to be around her now. She remembered uneasily the times when she had entered the room to serve tea and cookies. Conversation would suddenly cease, and she would feel their eyes upon her, critically examining every move she made.

It would be nice to have the house to myself for a week, she went on to herself, but if she does go, would she only come back more demanding and selfish than she is now? If she doesn't go, at least things can't get much worse than they already are. Finally, after days of indecision, the older woman packed a suitcase, dressed in her best kimono, and stepped out of the garden into the path that led to the street.

"Now, be sure you are careful about not using too much electricity, Sachiko, and do try to buy some decent fish for Ichiro to eat tonight." She paused uncertainly and turned to Kawaguchi San. "I wonder if I should go after all. There are so many things that could go wrong if I were not here."

"Sachiko San will get along just fine. Come, the taxi is waiting." Gently sliding the gate shut, Kawaguchi San took her arm. Sachiko could hear her mother-in-law muttering and complaining as she walked down the path to the street. The motor of the taxi roared as it turned around, its tires screeched, and then, finally, she knew she was alone in her husband's house for the first time since her marriage.

"What shall I do next?" she asked herself, savoring the deliciousness of the moment. To choose what you want to do, and then to be able to do it! To decide whether you will clean the house, wash the clothes, or just sit down and drink a cup of tea—suddenly the thought of it was almost too much. She sat down on the mat floor, hid her face in her hands, and thought about all that had happened.

Little sounds, sounds she had been too busy to hear for a long time, began to make their way to her ears. Sounds that belonged to the house—Shiro barking, the postman at the gate, the next-door neighbor talking with her baby—suddenly they all belonged to her and to her alone. She picked up the dishes on the table and carried them to the kitchen.

That morning she worked quickly and joyously, enjoying every minute of her work. It was no longer something she had to do. It became a part of her and the soothing quietness of the house. She waited until early afternoon when the daily fresh vegetables would have been brought from the market to the shops and then went to buy the things she would need for dinner that night. Finally, the house clean, the clothes dry, shopping done, and dinner partially prepared, she took her towel and soap and went to the public bathhouse for a long, hot bath.

"Tadaima!"

Ichiro! Sachiko looked at the clock on the kitchen shelf. *"Okaeri nasai!"* She dried her hands and hurried to the entrance.

"You're home early," she said, feeling strangely shy. He looked at her silently without answering. She felt the blood rush to her face and turned to take his briefcase and coat. "Your mother left about eleven this morning," she tried again, her voice faltering a little as she spoke.

"She's gone, is she?" He looked about him. Then his eyes returned to her face. "It's good to be alone."

The world stood still in that one moment. She was aware only that he was here and that he smiled at her, that his eyes caressed her. "Ichiro . . ." She stopped, forgetting what she had been about to say. Feeling foolishly gay, knowing that he had come home early because he had known that she was alone, she tried in vain to control the tingling in her body and the rapid beating of her heart. Then, with a soft cry, his coat clasped between them, she was in his arms and his face was against hers.

He held her tightly, and the sweet scent of her hair,

still damp from her bath, filled his nostrils. "This is my wife," he said to himself. "She belongs to me." If the nights he had spent in the tea houses haunted him, he drove them from his mind. Suddenly, he knew perfect peace. He was overcome by the thought that the thing for which he had been searching so long, that which he had gone elsewhere to seek, that which he had thought the geisha could give him, was here in his home and had belonged to him all the while. Slender and graceful, quietly ready to love him and to serve him, she was the only one who could give him the happiness for which he had longed.

"Why did I try to destroy the one thing that could make me happy?" he asked himself as his arms tightened around her. For the first time he asked the question honestly. He saw himself as he really was, and he did not like what he saw. He saw himself and he saw his mother. Remembering, he felt again the old shackles which bound him to her. His body became tense and his mind weary. The frown on her face as she had complained to him about his wife, the little lies she had manufactured to make him think that the girl was not concerned about him or his welfare—all these things he had seen, but had until this time refused to recognize.

"But she's my mother," one part of him cried. "Look what she did for me!" But his other self answered softly, "Yes, but look at what she is doing to you now." The nights when he had returned only to hear her whining and complaining, when his young wife had been kept busy with made-up work so that he hardly ever saw her, when the peace of his home was torn by rivalry for his time and attention—he thought of all of this now.

"But she's my mother," he kept insisting, unconscious that he cried aloud, shattering the silence of the mellow fall afternoon. Like glass, it seemed to tinkle when it broke and he became suddenly aware of his voice and of his wife's face close to his.

She clung to him while the tears filled her eyes and ran down her cheeks. He stood silently while her face brushed his, salty and wet against his lips.

"She's my mother," he repeated to himself thoughtfully, but a sudden light sparkled in his eyes. "But this is my wife and she needs me as well." He turned his face so that he could look into her eyes, and his voice became tender as he spoke to her. The flame sprang up in her eyes, drove the tears away, and reflected the intensity of his own feelings.

"Sachiko . . ." he said softly. He was saying more than just her name. He was saying more than just, "Let us have this one perfect week, then we'll have something to remember all our lives." He was trying to tell her he loved her, but the word love did not cross his lips easily. His need of her, his desperate need and love for her were included in the one word he spoke and she responded to that need. The flame burst, exploded, and enveloped them together. Suddenly he knew positively, without doubt, that he loved her. He loved her more than he had ever loved anyone before in all his life.

Later, after their dinner was finished and Shinobu was asleep in his bed, they sat on the veranda in the darkness and talked.

"I didn't realize what had happened," Ichiro was saying softly. "I think I tried to believe that whatever she would do would be right—just because she is my mother. I knew she had been right about so many things and made myself believe that she couldn't do wrong. There were times when I wondered if what she said was always true, but it was easier to believe her than to go against her."

She could see his face dimly in the light from the street lamp, but the expression on his face escaped her. Yet she was glad for the darkness, for with it there was no need to hide the naked feelings which showed on their faces as they talked about things they had never been able to talk about—as they faced themselves and their failings as they had never before faced them.

"What kind of person was your father, Ichiro?" she asked.

He sat thinking for a long time, and when he spoke it was a trifle uncertainly. "My strongest impressions of him are of kindness, quietness, and understanding. My mother was never quiet. She was always talking and telling us what to do. Yet, if I remember well enough, she usually did what he asked her to do."

"If he had lived, things would have been different."

"Yes, they would have been different." He paused. "For so long I was all Mother had. Father died and she lost her home, and Grandmother died soon afterward. I told myself that I owed it to her to be a good son. She had sacrificed for me, given up her own life in order that I might go to school, pushed me every evening to get my studying done, to take examinations for the best school I could, and to get the best job I could find. I didn't realize until just lately that she was doing it, not for my sake, but for her own. I'm sure she loves me, but I wonder if her concern about what she would do in her old age, how she would live, wasn't so great that she sometimes forgot what was best for me. I don't think she knows what she has done to us. She resents it when things don't go her own way, but then she has had her own way in my life as long as I can remember. I thought that I had to do everything her way. I thought it was the only way to pay her back for what she did for me.

"But now I'm beginning to wonder if there couldn't have been another way," he continued. "I wonder if there might not have been some way to find out what I wanted to do and to do it, but in such a manner that she wouldn't have been hurt." He shook his head in bewilderment. "I don't know. Perhaps the way we did it was the only way, considering the circumstances."

A bird chirped sleepily in the bamboo tree, and from

another tree somewhere near by its mate answered, low and chuckling. "The thing is, we can't go on as we have been. It is not good for us and it's not good for her. Yet I wonder if it's not too late to change her."

Sachiko looked up thoughtfully into his face, then out into the darkness of the garden. "It may be hard for her to change, but it is not too late for us."

He glanced at her swiftly. "What do you mean?"

What do I mean, she mused. I wonder if I really know. Can I explain to him so he will understand? Slowly, she began to put into words the things she had been thinking for the past year. Falteringly, a word at a time, she tried to say it so that he would not become offended. "For a long time, I thought it was her fault completely. I blamed her for everything that went wrong. Then someone helped me to see that I, too, was not blameless. I knew that I could not look at your mother and say, 'Well, if she won't stop hurting me, I will stop hurting her.' I began to feel that the only way for me to be happy was to get rid of my hatred and resentments. Then, even if she did not change her ways, I could find peace within myself."

"Where did you hear teachings such as that?"

"The missionary told us at the cooking class."

"It sounds good, but does it really work? Can you really love someone who resents you?"

Her voice was quiet. "I think you can." They were silent, then, listening to the night sounds and thinking of the past.

"It's hard on Shinobu, this feeling of tenseness and bickering," he said in a low voice. "Children don't understand, but they feel things without being told."

"I wish I knew what to do," Sachiko agreed. "Shinobu knows that when I ask him to do something, he only has to go to your mother and she will tell him that he doesn't have to do it. Yesterday, before he left for school, I asked him to brush his teeth, and he told me that Grandmother had told him that he didn't have to begin brushing them yet. As a result of her pampering he eats what he wants and whenever he wants to eat. She gives him candy before dinner almost every night. Then I have to scold him when he doesn't want to finish his rice."

"Of course you are more aware of that than she is. We do things differently now from the way they were done even twenty years ago when we were small."

"But at least she could show some respect for the fact that I am his mother."

"They don't, though. Older people very seldom think of that."

"And the other evening, when I wanted Shinobu to get ready for bed, she said, 'Oh, let him stay up for a while.' There he sat, listening to us argue whether he should go to bed or not. She said that it was good for him to watch television each night, broadened his outlook! Broadened his outlook for what, I wonder? *Sumo* wrestling? Is he preparing for the life of a cowboy? Or a jazz singer?" She sighed heavily.

"I know what you mean, but what can we do? She's my mother, and I don't think we should try to hurt her. Perhaps if we are patient for a while, she will begin to understand a little better."

Sachiko said nothing, for there was nothing else to say.

CHAPTER SEVENTEEN

SACHIKO WOULD NEVER forget the day she first smelled incense. Its sweetly pungent scent filled the house and drove out even the odor of the *omiso* soup.

"Incense," she said to herself, startled at the thought. "Why should there be the smell of incense?" She opened the door between the kitchen and the eating room. The room was empty and the *amado* were still undrawn, but through the slightly opened door of her husband's mother's room, a light flickered. As she watched, it faltered, then burned strongly again.

She crept to the door of the room. Her eyes, unaccustomed to the darkness of the room, could at first perceive only the candles that stood like sentinels before a large, boxlike *butsudan*. Then she saw that the Buddhist worship altar, so long unused, was now decorated with flowers and food—a dish of warm rice, an apple, and a can of peaches. In the center of the altar stood a large picture of her husband's dead father. Dressed formally in a black suit, his expression unsmiling, his forever young face looked at her out of the past. It brought the war, the years of sacrifice, the sadness of a home and a small boy without a father unbearably close to her.

Sachiko caught her breath. Before the altar, almost obscured by the smoke that rose about her, knelt the old woman. Her face was waxen in the dusky light. Her eyes were closed, and had it not been for the restless rubbing of her hands against a wooden rosary, Sachiko would have thought her asleep. Then her lips moved, and like the rustling of dry leaves in the fall, her whispering chant filled the room.

"Oh, God!" Sachiko clung to the doorframe. "Not this!" Her legs trembled as she slipped from the room to the familiarity of the kitchen. "Why should *Obaasan* think of the Buddha now?" she wondered aloud. "It has been a long time since she has even visited the temple, and the worship altar was only yesterday covered with dust. Is it because she is growing older and her mind turns to death? Or," she shuddered, "is it because I have become a Christian?" She picked up a dish, then set it down again. There will be more to come, she thought, struck with sudden fright. There will be tension and quarrelings, hatred and fear. Can we stand strong against it? She thought of Ichiro, loving him in spite of his weaknesses and understanding the control his mother had had over him all his life.

Several days later, after Sachiko had set the table for breakfast she went to find Shinobu to get him ready for school. She found him in his grandmother's room.

"Now, this is the way you bow, Shinobu Chan!" said the old woman from the floor where she knelt before the *butsudan*. "Come, you can do it."

"I don't want to bow to that old thing!"

Her lips tightened and her eyes grew cold. "I told you to bow!" she cried harshly, grabbing his arm and half pulling him down beside her.

"I don't want to! I don't want to!"

Sachiko watched from the doorway, her heart sick within her. The child's eyes were dry, but his lip trembled. "Oh, Mother, don't make him do it," she said before she could stop herself.

The woman glared at her from the floor, her eyes pits of hatred, her mouth a thin grim line in a white face. "What are you doing—spying on me?"

"No, really. I . . ."

"Spying on me so you can run to Ichiro and lie to him about me."

"*Okaasan,* please don't get excited . . ."

"Okaasan! Okaasan!" she mocked. "I'm not your mother. And I'm glad I wasn't the one to give birth to such as you." The blue veins on her face bulged, her lips hardly moved. "There has been a curse on this house ever since the day you came. Now you have brought a foreign religion here! Are the ways of your fathers not good enough for you?"

The room became very still. Sachiko sighed, a sharply drawn-in breath that shook her body. The child had long since escaped to the hallway. He waited there, his eyes wide with terror. She turned and put her arm around his trembling body.

The old woman's hoarse breathing rose to a scream. "If you leave this room now, all the gods in hell will not be able to save you. I'll have you driven from this house, and the whole neighborhood will know why you left!"

A whimper sprang from the throat of the child. "Mother, come! Please come! I must get ready for kindergarten."

The clock in the kitchen ticked on relentlessly. The time passed, but still she stood there, knowing that she had no choice but to wait until the old woman's anger had spent itself. "Shinobu, run outside and wait for a while. Mother will get your breakfast soon."

"I won't! I won't!" Four months of love and care on her part had not yet erased the years of neglect. He kicked and screamed until finally she held him, sobbing against her. Above the cries of the child rose the terrible anger of her mother-in-law.

"Give up your foreign religion," the older woman ordered harshly. "Pay your respects to the gods of your husband's ancestors!"

Sachiko could not speak.

"Show the child how to bow, then, if you know so well."

Still, Sachiko said nothing.

"Pay your respects to your ancestors!" she said again with deadly quiet.

She wants me to worship the Buddha, Sachiko thought. Give up the joy and peace I've found in Christ. She wants me to return to the terror and darkness of unbelief. Unbelief in anything. For the Buddha would not satisfy me, now. After knowing the Christ, the Buddha could never be real to me.

But was it right that she should be the cause of strife in the home? Would it be better for the child if he were not to see scenes like this—even if it meant that he would never grow up knowing the love of his mother and the warm arms of the church?

Death would be preferable to that, she thought. If I had lived during the times of my fathers, she went on bitterly to herself, I could have chosen death through harakiri—a knife thrust in my stomach, blood staining a white kimono. She shook her head dully. This was not the way to think. A Christian does not commit suicide.

"If I gave You up, my God, I could not live any longer." As she prayed, her mind cleared and her arm became firm and steady around the body of the child. "Life without You would be worse than death. I cannot give You up," she prayed passionately. "Even if I am killed, You must be first in my life. If I am driven from my home, I cannot betray You, my Lord." She looked at the candlelit altar, the incense still filling the air with its acrid odor. It was a simple thing her mother-in-law asked her to do. She must only bow before the altar. She need not believe it in her heart—simply bow.

"But if I bow before the Buddha, I will know that I have done wrong. The evil will come from within me, not from the outside." Her lips moved, but no sound passed through them.

"If you bow every morning," her mother-in-law said almost pleadingly, "I will leave you alone. You may still believe your Christian foolishness and go to your foreign church. Do this, I ask you, so that evil will not come to our house."

"But I can't," Sachiko cried passionately. "I can't bow before a Buddhist altar. I am a Christian!"

Before the words were out of her mouth, the blow caught her squarely across her face. She staggered and caught the doorframe to keep herself from falling, unaware of the blood on her lips. A deep, overwhelming consciousness of pity swept over her as she watched the other woman's face. The child cried out, and she hushed him gently.

"You think you can go against me?" Yoshiko Suzuki's face was the face of a *hyottokomen* mask, but it lacked the playfully pursed mouth and the laughing eyes. It was as white as the powdered countenance of a bride or of a geisha, but it had neither the sweetness of the young bride nor the adaptability of the geisha.

"You think you can go against me," the older woman started to say again, when a look of surprise crossed her face. This time, when her glance met Sachiko's, it was one of pleading, a desperate appeal for help. She staggered and would have fallen had Sachiko not caught her. "I'm sick," she whispered, unbelief filling her eyes.

Her body doubled up when the pain seized it, and then for just a moment Sachiko saw her mother-in-law's eyes. The hatred was gone. The bright, hard light of battle had disappeared. In its place was only resignation and defeat. She turned her head from the Buddhist altar, and for just a moment she looked Sachiko full in the face.

"So this is the way you win?" she said calmly and clearly. Then her lips twisted and her head fell against the young woman's body.

Sachiko laid her gently on the mat floor, and kneeling beside her, touched her hands. Then, seized suddenly with a kind of cold fear, she stood looking down at the woman before her, unable to move, struck dumb by her terror. Death, you've won! Or was it she, Sachiko, who was winning? Winning, not through her own goodness or love, as she had wanted to win her mother-in-law, but by the intervention of something stronger than herself.

"This isn't the way I wanted it," she cried, shuddering. "I wanted her to be happy. I wanted her to love me."

The child cried again and she came to herself. I've got to get a doctor, she thought wildly. After a swift glance again at the old woman's face, she grasped the child's hand and went through the garden to the neighbor's house for help.

They fought for her life, fought to bring her back to them. Again the months beside a hospital bed. Months of pills and medicines, and of a little boy who cried at night for his mother. Then little by little, the old woman began to return to them. But this time when death deserted her body, it did not leave her eyes. When she returned to the house, she sat for long hours looking out into the garden, her thoughts in some far-off place where Sachiko and her husband and child could not go. When she spoke, it was always of the past or of death.

"Remember, Ichiro, the cherry blossoms in Koganei? And how we went each year to see them? It was always so crowded with people, but we managed to find a place under the same tree every year." She laughed. "And how your father drank too much sake? We almost had to carry him when we returned home." She laughed again, but a look of puzzlement crossed her face. "Ichiro, where is your father? He didn't come home today, did he?"

Her son smiled to hide the pain in his eyes. When he did not answer at once, she asked him again impatiently.

"Mother," he said at last in a changed voice, low and slightly uneven, "remember what you told me one time? How Father would always be with us, taking care of us, watching over us?"

Her eyes became glazed once again. "Oh, yes," she said dully, "he was killed, wasn't he?" And again her mind was gone from them and she did not speak for several hours.

Sachiko's heart ached for them both. But there was little that she could do except care for the body that still lived and to communicate with the old woman at times when her mind became clear.

Several weeks later, Sachiko sat on the floor of her mother-in-law's room. The weather had turned cold and the evening, although it was not late, had already become dark. Outside the window she heard the laughter of Shinobu and Ichiro, and she knew that soon it would be the little boy's bedtime.

She laid her hands firmly on the slack, wasted flesh of her husband's mother, massaged her shoulders and then doubled her fists and pounded at the places where the muscles were tight.

Suddenly the paper-thin eyelids opened, and for the first time since her illness, she looked directly at Sachiko and knew her.

"Sachiko."

"Yes, *Okaasan.*"

"You are good." Her eyes closed again, and for a long time only the sound of young hands against aged flesh could be heard in the room. "I was think . . ." she said at last, then her voice faltered. She became silent. "I was thinking," she began again, "of something that happened."

"Yes, *Okaasan,*" Sachiko said again gently.

"It was the *butsudan,* wasn't it? The *butsudan* that caused the trouble?"

Sachiko shivered. Why, of all things, did she have to remember the incident that had caused her second heart attack? Uneasily she asked herself, What is she trying to do? What is she trying to get me to say? The scene flooded back into her mind and she knew with horror that she would never forget it.

"Why did you not bow before the *butsudan?*"

Sachiko was so deeply absorbed in her own thoughts that for a moment she did not hear what the other woman said. It was only when the older woman repeated it, when Sachiko felt her eyes upon her, that she caught the words. A faint, slow flush mounted into her soft, young face. Not trusting her voice to answer, she sat silently, her hands in her lap and her eyes on the floor.

Yoshiko Suzuki cleared her throat roughly. "You don't have to be afraid of me! I'm not going to hurt you now!"

Sachiko fought down the wild beating of her heart. When she spoke, her voice was low and hesitant. "I'm not afraid of you, *Okaasan.*"

"Well, there is no reason to be afraid."

"The reason I did not bow is that I am a Christian," she said at length. She raised her eyes and looked directly into the older woman's face. "Christians do not worship Buddha."

"You do not worship the Japanese Shinto gods either?"

"No, we do not worship them."

"Then what do you do when sickness comes? Does the Christian's God take care of you?"

"We believe that He does protect and care for us." Sachiko leaned forward earnestly, forgetting her fear. "For a long time, I did not understand about the Christian God. I didn't know that he loved me as a father loves his child—loved me even though I didn't believe in him and did not worship him. But I liked the teachings of the Christians. I liked to think that it is possible for people to be kind, to forget their own troubles and help others with theirs. When the missionary taught of

God's love and showed that we, too, must love, I thought it was good."

"But what do they worship? Do they have some symbol that they can see or keep in their homes?"

"No, we say that we do not need them, for our God is with us in our hearts. Our God is spirit."

The old woman stirred restlessly. "That sounds strange." She sat up slowly. "But to love others—to be always kind—such a teaching is good." Then, frowning slightly, she said with emphasis, "But a foreign religion! How can you forsake your own country's religions and take to another? For a thousand years our ancestors have worshiped Buddha and the Japanese gods. It must be a strange person, indeed, who would go against her own kind!" She sat, lost in thought, her face strangely softened, but her eyes alert. Then again, the shadow passed over them and she lay down and slept.

But just as Sachiko left the room, she heard the old woman murmur to herself, "Love and peace? Who knows? What if she is right?"

There was a long silence. The girl stood quietly, her hand on the door. Then again she heard, "But it is a foreign religion. I am too close to being with my ancestors to even think . . . too old . . . too sick!"

That evening the whole house slept deeply. The old woman slept, her mouth open and slack, while she dreamed her dreams of the past. She was a girl again, graceful, proper, and attractive. She waited by the side of her parents for her fiancé, whom she had never seen, but for whom she hoped she would learn to care. He came, and he was all she had wanted. Then somehow, he became mixed up in her dreams with her son, and love saturated with pain filled her sleeping world.

In the darkness of the young couple's room, Sachiko and her husband slept, and the sound of their breathing was mingled with the child's soft breath. The young man and his wife slept with their faces turned toward each other, as if, even in the depths of sleep, they loved and were conscious only of each other. The child held the edge of the *futon* comfortingly against his face, the edge ragged from its frequent contact with his hands and face.

They slept, and so they did not hear the wood tapper who made his rounds every night warning them, warning the community to watch their fires and to put them out before they went to bed. The hollow sound of his tapping faded away down the street, and still they slept, unheeding, unknowing.

They slept, and so they did not see the small flicker of flame which reached tentatively forward in the pit beneath the table. They did not see it reach again and again and again. They did not know that it sought for something on which to feed, nor did they see the smoke that soon rose from the blanket, the corner of which had fallen into the pit.

They slept. And while they slept, the flame greedily ate its way into the *tatami*.

CHAPTER EIGHTEEN

THE *osembei* SHOPKEEPER saw the fire from the upper story of his house above the rice cooky shop. He had locked the windows and drawn the heavy shutters over the front of the shop earlier in the evening. Then, enjoying the stillness of the night and knowing that his family were asleep in their beds upstairs, he had sat reading under a one-bulb light hanging from the ceiling in the little four-mat room at the back of the shop. He was a heavy-set man who said little, but he enjoyed his shop and his home more than anything else in the world. Though the hours were long, he would not have exchanged work with anyone.

The clock in the corner directed its fingers toward the eleventh hour. He stood up and stretched his pudgy hands as far above his head as he could. Time to go to bed. Another day tomorrow. He opened the door to the shop, looked about him with satisfaction at the neat square trays full of cookies and candy, the empty bread case which would in the morning be filled with freshly baked bread and rolls, the shelves of odds and ends—soap, toothbrushes, pins. Then, flicking off the light, he mounted the narrow stairs to the living area above. He slipped off his clothes in the dark and put on a cotton sleeping kimono. Drawing a heavy, padded kimono over the cotton one, he stepped over the sleeping body of his youngest born and made his way to the window above the street.

The city spread out before him in a rainbow of colors. Down the street toward the train station the lights were pink and blue, while beyond toward the Air Base he could see the bright reds, greens, and yellows, as well as the white lights which lined the runway. It was a cold night, sparkling and clear. He drew in his breath roughly, and the fresh air made him shiver.

A busy city in the daytime. But so quiet tonight! People call it a bad city. They say it is not a good place to live, so close to the Base. He drew the kimono closer to his face, thrust his hands into the wide sleeves. But it's my city. It's my home, and I like it, he thought, feeling a rush of affection for its tumbling bustle, the busses that pulled out of the parking places near the station every few minutes, the sound of the jets warming up out at the Base, the chatter of Americans, the staccato sound of the language of his own people. He even felt a certain tolerance for the hundreds of bars which dotted the roads surrounding the Base, the blaring rock and roll which blasted the air before their doorways, the taxis weaving back and forth across the town from the Base to the train station, then back to the Base, and on to the station again. "It's my city," he said aloud, "it's my big, bad city."

Suddenly he saw the flame. The smile on his face froze. Only his eyes moved, and as they moved, thoughts whirled frantically across his mind. A fire! A tiny flicker of hot flame licked its way around the edge of the *amado* on the house across the street, then disappeared. He thought foolishly, I've been seeing things, stayed up too late, and turned to enter his bed. But something drew his eyes to the ground, and when he saw it again, this time a little brighter, a little gayer, he knew that wishing could not make it go away.

"Fire!" A brilliant, furious enemy, hated and feared by all the people of Japan. Hated and feared by a people who lived in wood houses with heavy paper doors, houses crowded together so that they became tinder for any small flame not watched and guarded with fear.

"Fire!" The cry was enough to send his household from their sleep out into the night. It was enough to make the most innocent person shiver in his bed. It was enough to make the strong weak and the weak hysterical. Gathering his kimono about his body, the *osembeya san* ran down the narrow stairs, slid his feet into wooden clogs which waited for him at the bottom, and ran out into the night to cry the alarm. The swift sound of a man's running, the sound of wooden *geta* on the streets, awakened the community to its nightmare. The hush of the night fled with the running of other *geta* and the clamoring of the voices of the neighborhood.

A cold wind was born that night. It began to chase itself around the corners and through the tops of the tall crytomeria pines. The bamboo bent themselves low to the ground, then sprang up again after it passed, only to be bent again when the next flurry caught them. It struck the face of the noodle man. He pulled his jacket closer around his neck, set his hat more securely on his head and continued on his slow way up the street between the houses. The light on his cart was a little oasis of brightness in the dark of the night. It cast a soft shadow on his face, emphasized the loneliness, the weird mystery of the sound of his whistle. Not just the usual whistle such as a *tofu* man would use in the mornings and evenings when he made his rounds selling bean curd—the whistle of the noodle man was almost a song.

When the people heard the noodle man's whistle, it was always at night, many times at midnight, and it had a lonely sad sound. They bought the noodles, ate them steaming hot while they sat in padded kimonos and warmed their hands at a *hibachi* pot. But as they ate, they also remembered the old man's face. They remembered that he was always alone and cold. The sound of the whistle stayed with them for a long time.

Sometimes children would wake at night, hearing the mourning of the noodle man's whistle. They would wake and run to the window to watch the flickering light move slowly down the street. At times a child would cry softly, "Poor little noodle man, so cold and so lonely!" Then, looking up at his mother's face, he would smile and say, "I like the noodle man, *Okaasan!*" And the mother would smile, remembering the days past when she, too, had run to the window, a child barely able to reach it, to be lifted up by her mother to see the noodle man pass.

The noodle man was aware of only one thing—that soon he could stop his work for the night and return to sit beside the warm charcoal pot in his home. "Sometime," he said bitterly to himself, "I'm going to quit and get a job somewhere else. If I were younger, I'd try to find one at the Base. But this walking, walking, walking, and then, hardly a noodle sold!" He yanked his collar up around his face and pushed on through the darkened streets.

He stepped aside when the fire engines passed. And as he waited for the sirens to die away, his face passive, eyes partially covered by heavy lids, the bitterness in his heart disappeared. For that moment he was thankful to be a noodle man, thankful to be alive. Tightening his grip on the handle of his cart, he turned his face toward his home.

"I'm quitting," he said to himself. "I'm quitting for the night." The light on his cart bobbed once more in the wind before he turned the corner.

Across the city, Emile Roberts stirred in her bed. A fire! Somewhere there is a fire tonight and someone will be out in the cold watching his home burn. The little things about one's home, they will all be gone. The photograph albums, school books, clothes, a favorite dress or jacket or a priceless kimono. She burrowed her head under the covers, felt the warmth of her big husband beside her, snuggled against his slumbering body. Carried on the wind, wavering, crying, now smothered, now loud and clear, the scream of the fire engines brought uneasiness to all who heard.

How good it feels to be here in one's bed! How warm it is! How safe I feel! But somewhere, someone is not safe, is not warm, is not in his bed. "God, keep them safe. Keep them from the fire. Give them comfort," she prayed as the sirens died away into the night. For a long time she lay thinking—thinking of Bobby who lay in his bed in the next room. Thinking of her husband and of herself, of their work in a country not their own, but now their second home. "God, keep us safe," she prayed again, suddenly remembering the distance that lay between their home in the outskirts of Tokyo and their parents' homes in America. "Keep us safe, but more than that, help us to be used and useful in Your work here in Japan."

When she slept again she dreamed, not of the fire engines, nor of the wind that blew that night; she dreamed of a high, sunny hill and of cherry blossoms which fell like snow from the dark branches of the trees. A gentle breeze blew the blossoms into the air and sent them scurrying to the ground. She walked beneath the arch formed by the trees, and the sun was warm on her shoulders.

The fire cast flickering shadows on the ground. A red and yellow demon, it raged and leaped from the windows, tore at the roof until it fell with a crash, sending sparks into the air. It lit the faces of the crowd standing in hushed awe, caught the naked thoughts that showed on their faces. It betrayed the terror-stricken ones, the self-satisfied ones who were glad that if a fire had to come it had come to some house other than their own. It revealed greed, shock, fear, panic, and pity.

The face of Matsuoka was still. Even her eyes did not move and she seemed almost in a trance. She stood clutching her kimono about her, unaware of the wind which tore through her hair. Her laughing, usually gay face was painfully quiet and her tongue stilled.

The next-door neighbors—the Tanaka family—stood in a row watching the flames. The youngest child cried and clutched his mother's clothes. The oldest, Keiko, the promise of beauty shining in her clear face and bright eyes, stood pale and silent beside her brothers. She, more than almost anyone else, with the sensitiveness that comes with youth, was aware of tragedy. She searched with her eyes until she found the ones she was looking for. Then her eyes, too, were still.

A grandmother clutching her cane, a school child with bare feet thrust hurriedly into *geta,* a workman with a beard heavy on his face—they were people who lived in the community. People who lived with and who knew the Suzuki family. They knew more than Sachiko or her husband or her mother-in-law realized they knew. Rumor traveled fast and houses were close together. So now, some came to sympathize. Some came to receive vindication. Some came to say, "A curse was on that house. The evil has done its work." But all came to watch, because in Japan nothing is private, nothing really belongs to oneself alone—not even tragedy.

Sachiko kicked the *futon* aside, turned restlessly in her bed. "It's hot." Her head ached. A throbbing pain ran down the back of her neck and on down her body. "It's hot," she said to herself again, sitting up dazedly. She wiped her eyes and sat for a moment while uneasiness stole over her.

Something is wrong, she thought suddenly. Something is not the same. A peculiar smell of smoke? A noise from the eating room? She rose to her feet silently and tip-toed to the door of the room. When she opened it the heat and smoke almost overcame her. Fire! The house is on fire!

"Ichiro!" She opened her mouth to call, but no sound came out. Swallowing hard, swallowing the fear that was in her throat, she forced herself to scream. The smoke curled into the room from under the half-open door, while above her the shriek of the wind joined the crackling of the flames in the other room. Then she felt her husband's body against hers and heard Shinobu's cries.

"Take the boy outside," Ichiro was shouting at her. At first his words had no meaning. Then somehow, her mind dull with terror, she drew herself back. Picking up the child, she carried him to the *genkan*. For just a moment she turned to look at the blazing room. In that moment she saw with horror her mother-in-law's face, twisted, crying, calling for help. She saw her standing in the doorway of her room, while between them the flames rose to the roof. She saw her for only a second, then the face was gone and the flames covered the space in the doorway.

"Ichiro! Your mother!"

"I'll get her. You go on outside with Shinobu!"

She watched him go. She watched until she could see him no longer. Then, turning, she staggered from the house to the garden, and fell into the arms of her friends.

When she saw her husband again, his face was black from the smoke and his eyes were bleak. Behind them lay the ruins of their home, a charred mass of memories. The happy times they had had there together, the disappointments, the tensions and sorrows—they were all gone now. Memories. Now, only memories.

Then her eyes were drawn by the huddled lump of flesh and bones which lay at her feet, the shell which had once held the soul and spirit of her mother-in-law. Dead! And there was no joy at her death, only a terrible kind of grief. Sorrow for the happy times that had been few. Grief because there had never been a chance for understanding or love, disappointment because the relationship that might have been good had held hatred and controversy.

"Dead!" she repeated, her voice dull, her eyes dry, her chest heavy.

Her husband crouched on the ground, his head in his hands. She touched his shoulder gently, bent to pick up the child, and held him against her so hard that he cried. Absently drying his tears, caressing his body, she turned her eyes on the dying embers of her home.

CHAPTER NINETEEN

THEY FOUND AN APARTMENT not far from their community and moved the few things which had been saved from the fire into the two small four-mat rooms.

"It's only for a little while," Ichiro said, trying to smile as he looked about him. "As soon as we can save a little money, we can build again." The smile struggled but did not quite succeed in reaching his eyes. A teacher's salary did not leave extras on which to build a new house, and the insurance on the old one was not enough to make even a beginning. "It's only for a little while . . ." he repeated again, his voice flat and lifeless.

It was a closet of an apartment, set in the noise and bustle of twenty other units. All were gathered together in a large wooden building and were connected by long, dark, dirt-floor halls. Outside the children tumbled roughly on the grassless, shrubless ground, long since stamped bare by hundreds of children's feet. Even the branches of the trees were broken, the ground about them trampled hard. At night the sound of the children's crying or laughing or quarreling filtered through the thin wooden walls. It became a nightmarish echo of their own child's cries—nighttime crying which had begun again and had continued since the fire.

Sachiko cooked their meals on a little gas hot plate, kept the dishes and food in a small cupboard, for there was no kitchen. She said little, but her hands spoke gently for her when she smoothed the perspiration from the child's forehead or when she helped her husband take off his coat upon his return.

The funeral was over, and also the rollicking, drunken reception held for friends and relatives. The funeral was over—the chanting of the priest before an altar decorated with fruit, candles, and flowers set up in the house of her friend Matsuoka. Set up in a borrowed room, for they had had no home in which to entertain their guests. The smell of incense, the large paper flowers set on long stilts wrapped in black and white, the agony of waiting in the reception room of the crematorium while not far away the bones and flesh of her husband's mother burned and crackled; then the formality of picking out the bones with chopsticks, the return to Matsuoka's home, and more long hours of sake and food and merrymaking—it was all past. They had observed the forty-nine days required of them to preserve their mother's memory—the forty-nine days of darkness, after which they had taken the urn with her bones to the cemetery and buried them. The funeral was over. She was dead. But she was not forgotten.

They had not forgotten her, for they had had to borrow money for her funeral and it would not be fully repaid for many months, perhaps years. They had not forgotten her, for they knew now that they loved her and missed her, missed even the sharpness of her sarcasm. They had not forgotten, for every day they asked themselves, "What did we do wrong? What could we have done differently? Perhaps if we had been a little kinder . . ." And every evening when he returned home from his work, Sachiko searched her husband's face for some glimmer of hope. But each day his face seemed thinner and his eyes more dull. Despondency settled over them like an evil cloud, and she knew that soon she would have to speak the thoughts that were in her own heart.

She found him one evening by the window looking out at the winter bleakness. He watched the children who played outside the window, their faces red and chapped from the wind. Then his eyes moved to a small boy who stood by himself in the far corner of the yard. His eyes were wide and dark, his face pinched and blue.

Loneliness was a bridge that bound the three of them together—himself, the girl, and this child. The child who was called Shinobu.

She came to him and stood beside him. He felt her shoulder brush his arm and turned his head. For a long moment their eyes met, then desolately his returned to the scene outside.

"It will get better," she said softly, knowing of the heaviness that lay within him. "Soon, it will get better."

He did not answer at once. He was thinking of the times that had been, of the home that was now ashes, of the peacefulness of the garden—the garden where they no longer walked and talked together. He thought of his mother's face, proud and ambitious and of how they would never see it again. "Better?" he said at last, his voice low and filled with bitterness. "It will have to get better, for nothing could be worse than this." His glance took in the dusty yard, the worn *tatami* mats, and the dark, dingy room.

She caught the echo of resentment in his voice and her heart ached. "But we have each other," she answered simply.

He said nothing for a moment, but his eyes softened and the frown disappeared from his face. He looked down at her and tenderness filled his face. "Yes, we have each other," he said at length in a changed voice, low as her own. "We have each other. We have not always had that."

They sat in silence for a while, thinking of the time when moments with each other had to be stolen. He looked at her clear, finely molded face and called to mind the times when his hands had traced the lines of her nose and jaw or he had felt the softness of her hair against his skin.

"If I had had all the freedom in the world," she said softly and happily, "I would not have exchanged it for the years I have spent in our home with you."

He did not answer her. He was seized with wonder at

her kindness and her lack of resentment for the years when she had been little more than a servant for his mother.

"We have so much to live for," she went on, and her smile lit her whole face. "We are young. It will not take long to pay back the money we owe, then we can begin working toward the building of our home."

"But the child—Shinobu!" he said after a moment. "What will happen to him while we are waiting for that time? We can sacrifice for it and it will be hard, but it will not break us. But a little child . . ."

"He will get used to it," she said. "He will become used to it, and it will be all right if we are careful. He was not accustomed to having his own way before he came to live with us. It may be easier for him than it is for us. We have had too much given to us."

At her words he looked searchingly into the past. He thought of his mother's face during the war years and after the death of his father. It had become thin, but the eyes had remained alive and full of determination. The ambition in those eyes had followed him all during the years he had struggled through examinations for entrance into good schools. They followed him now, even after her death—haunted him so that he could not forget them.

"My mother did too much for me. She lived her life through me."

"She loved you," the young girl answered.

"Yes," he repeated, "she did love me. But it would have been better if she had not loved me so much." The past was close about them. The dark rooms were gone and they walked together through the garden beside the house. Inside, his mother would be sewing and her thoughts would be on him.

"But if she had only loved me a little," the girl said and pain was in her voice. "I wanted her to love me as a daughter. I wanted to be a daughter to her. Instead, I was a source of sorrow and embarrassment."

Her distress aroused him, and he turned toward her and held her lightly. "I think she did love you. I think she did not want to, but she could not help it."

She stood sunk in her own thoughts, gazing into the distance.

He shook her slightly, forced her face tenderly up so that she looked into his eyes. "Sachiko, she did love you. Let me tell you how I know." For a moment he was silent as he groped for the right words. "One day soon after her last illness, after she had returned home from the hospital," he began, "I found her in her room looking through your old photo album." His words came slowly, and more than once in the course of his story he had to stop to collect his thoughts. "She looked up at me and said, 'I have always wanted a daughter of my own, but since that wasn't possible, it was good that you married someone like Sachiko.' "

He did not go on to tell her the rest of his mother's words, but they returned to his mind now and he stood silently remembering them. "Sachiko will be good to you after I am gone. She is a Christian and Christians are not known for cruelty. I can rest easier knowing that she will be a good wife for you." Had she known she was to die? Perhaps she did, for during those few weeks before her death the sweetness which he had remembered in her face during his childhood had returned to it. Peace had been in the house again, but it was a peace that was mixed with a premonition of death and the possibility of more illness.

Sachiko stirred a little in his arms, but did not speak at once. His words took her back to a cold winter night when her mother-in-law had asked her so pointedly about her faith in Christ. And again the words she had heard murmured as she left the room echoed in her mind, "Perhaps she is right. Who knows? But I am too close to my ancestors . . ."

"Love," she said wonderingly. "We are taught that

that word is one of the most important of all words. Another one is peace."

"We?" he queried. "Who is we?"

"We who are Christians." Her voice was low and gentle.

He was silent, apparently lost in what she had said. When at last he spoke, his voice was hesitant and unsure. "Before you became a Christian, I had never known one before. I still don't understand what you believe, but it seems good for a man to have some faith to live by."

"Your mother worshiped Buddha."

"Yes, but I don't think she was satisfied. She remembered Buddha only when she was in trouble, and still she was unhappy." He moved away from her, crouched beside the round *hibachi* heater, warmed his hands over the glowing charcoal. His forehead wrinkled thoughtfully. "There must be something that could give peace and happiness even though everything is not easy or just as we want it. It seems that faith should be more than just a means of getting what we ask."

She sank down to the mat floor beside him. "It is," she said slowly. "Christianity does much more than that for a person."

"Gives peace and happiness even in something like this?" His eyes took in the room, the pitifully small pile of their possessions, harbored in the wooden cupboard.

"Yes," she said softly, "even in the midst of troubles such as we have had."

For a long time he sat silent with the ring of her voice in his ear. "I was thinking," he said at last, "of Shinobu and of how his face looked when he sang in the kindergarten Christmas program. He really believes what they teach him, doesn't he?"

"He is a child," she said after a moment. "He probably believes what he understands. But he does love his kindergarten—the teachers, the minister, or anyone who is in any way associated with it."

"Then he will probably follow the Christian way when he grows older," Ichiro continued. They sat in silence for a while, thinking of the child, his tumbled hair, his gay, teasing smile. Then another picture crossed their minds—a picture of a lonely, cold little boy standing on the edge of a circle of shabby, noisy boys and girls.

"If we are to make him really happy, we must stand together. The three of us must be one," he went on slowly, thoughtfully. "It is not good for a family to be divided."

Sensing that he was making some decision, that he was struggling to make up his mind, she waited for him to speak, her eyes fixed on his face.

"If the old way did not make my mother happy," he said, his voice suddenly sure and strong, "perhaps the new way is best."

"The new way?"

He looked into her face, smiled a little, and then his glance fell to his hands. When he looked up at her again, his face was slightly flushed, but his eyes were steady. "Yes, the new way—the Christian way."

Joy spread through her, smoothing away the tangle of worry and concern. She felt warmed and at peace. For just a moment she closed her eyes to hide the tears. "We will learn together," she whispered.

"We will learn together," he repeated.

The door opened softly, and the child stepped into the room. They arose and drew him close to them, and the circle was completed. He looked up at their faces, his eyes puzzled. But when he saw them smile, he, too, smiled, and the warmth spread through him.

"The winter is almost over," Sachiko murmured softly. "When the winter is gone, the spring will come. And with the spring comes the dawning."

"And with the dawning, the peace of a new day—of a new life," the boy's father finished for her.

"The peace of a new life . . ." the two of them repeated softly. Not understanding, but liking the sound of it, the child echoed the words, "A new life . . . a new life."